MW00564027

CANDLE IN THE DARK

& OTHER STORIES

MARK ALLEN BOONE

CANDLE IN THE DARK
& OTHER STORIES

MARK ALLEN BOONE

Echelon House Publishing
River Forest, IL

Candle in the Dark and Other Stories
©2021 by Mark Allen Boone
All Rights Reserved
Published by Echelon House Publishing
401 William Street #6273
River Forest, IL 60305

Queries regarding rights and permissions should be addressed to:
Echelon House Publishing Co. at www.echelonhousepublishing.com.

Manufactured in the United States of America
Interior Design by: Arlana Johnson
Cover Design by: Designs by Triv
Publisher's Cataloging-In-Publication Data
(Prepared by The Donohue Group, Inc.)

Names: Boone, Mark Allen, author.
Title: Candle in the dark and other stories / Mark Allen Boone.
Description: River Forest, IL : Echelon House Publishing, [2021] | Some stories previously published in various books and magazines.
Identifiers: ISBN 9780977251520 (paperback)
Subjects: LCSH: African Americans--Illinois--Chicago--Social conditions--Fiction. | West Side (Chicago, Ill.)--Social conditions--Fiction. | City dwellers--Illinois--Chicago--Social conditions--Fiction. | LCGFT: Short stories.
Classification: LCC PS3552.O64384 C36 2021 | DDC 813/.54--dc23

ISBN: 978-0-9772515-2-0

"Candle in the Dark," Winner of the 1975 Triton College New Writers Workshop Award for Best Short Story was first published in *AIM Magazine*, Vol. 7, Number 3, Fall 1980
"Beatitude" was first published as "Brunswick Stew" in *West Side Stories*, edited by George Bailey, City Stoop Press, 1992, Chicago.
"A Qualified Prospect" was first published as "The Prospect" in *AIM Magazine*, Vol.9, Number Two, Summer 1982.
"Day Work" was first published as "Swan Song" in *AIM Magazine*, Vol.14, Number Three, Spring 1985
"A Mortgage Burning Party" was first published in *Guildworks: Writings by the West Side Writers Guild*, Blacksmith Press, 1996.
"The Derelict" was first published in *Guildworks: Writings by the West Side Writers Guild*, Blacksmith Press, 1996.

To Ruth Mays Apilado

Table of Contents

Preface

IN 1970, on a visit to the Henry Legler Regional Branch Library at 115 S. Pulaski Road, one of Chicago's three regional public libraries, which I frequented growing up, I browsed the section of a small room devoted to black writers. At the time, I had no aspirations of becoming a writer myself; that is, until I happened upon a collection of short stories that featured on its cover a courtly, bespectacled, middle-aged African American man impeccably dressed in a dark suit standing next to the traffic light at the 47th Street CTA bus stop. The image arrested me before I noticed the title on the cover—*The Beach Umbrella*—and its author, Cyrus Colter.

Leafing through its contents, I was captivated by the subjects of the stories: ordinary African Americans who went about their lives in relative obscurity on Chicago's South Side facing everyday challenges with grace and pluck, hidden from the view of the larger mainstream society. So fascinated was I by stories that ranged from the black *haute monde* to the struggling *hoi polloi*, that I devoured them, losing myself in the characters and marveling at the spot-on descriptions, the authentic dialogue, and realism of the settings.

These people were *real* to me. People whom I had seen, lived amongst and grown up with. It then occurred to me that if he could immortalize in fiction the rhyme and rhythm of life on the South Side of Chicago, that perhaps I might be able to do the same for the maligned and often dismissed West Side.

Only later did I notice that the stories were so masterfully written that Colter, a lawyer who began to write as a weekend hobby at age fifty, was awarded the 1970 Iowa School of Letters Award for Short Fiction. Thus began my resolve to capture and rescue from obscurity the lives of ordinary West Siders who had heretofore not merited a passing glance in the published fiction of Chicago.

I studied Colter's stories in earnest for technique and style, eagerly awaited the publication of his first novel *The Rivers of Eros*, and then absorbed each subsequent one: *The Hippodrome*, the massive *Night Studies*, and his final one, *The Chocolate Soldier*. Eventually, when he joined the faculty of Northwestern University's Department of English three years later, I arranged a meeting with him, one that would prove to be highly auspicious for my writing career.

Fortunately for me, he was as gracious and forthcoming about his craft as he appeared to be on the cover of his collected stories. Afterwards, he gave me a copy of the *Chicago Review* that contained one of his latest stories, "The Frog Hunters," to add to my collection of his work. I left with him a copy of my short story, "Candle in the Dark," to which he promptly responded with a kind note that read: "This is a publishable story. Send it out." And send it out I did, only to be met with rejection after rejection from the nation's literary magazines.

Two years later in 1975, after had I enrolled in Triton College's New Writer's Workshop led by H.V.B. (Vivian) Halliburton, who later became a mentor and publicist for me and one of my most enthusiastic supporters, "Candle in the Dark" won first prize for short fiction.

The story about Aaron Cates, an elderly welfare recipient whose electric service has been cut off and who gets no sympathy from the welfare department or ComEd, faces a choice between breaking the lock on his meter, poaching electricity, or living by candlelight until the service could be restored. Ultimately, he does the right thing and, "With a strong puff of air, he blew it out, throwing the two-room apartment into total darkness before he undressed himself and wearily climbed into bed."

The story wasn't published until the fall of 1980, when Vivian Halliburton met Ruth Apilado, publisher of *AIM Magazine*, a quarterly that fostered racial harmony and peace. Ruth was promoting the magazine and thrust a copy into Vivian's hands. Perusing its contents, Vivian advised me to send my story "Candle in the Dark" to *AIM*. The magazine published the story, and, grateful for its acceptance, my association with *AIM* as its fiction editor began, a tenure than lasted 26 years. Unbeknownst to me at the time, Ruth Apilado (who, in recent years, at the age of 113, was designated one of the nation's supercentenarians), happened to be a close friend of Lydia Bosley, one of the teachers from my elementary school.

After the publication of "Candle," the succession of stories that comprise this collection followed as I wrote in the spare time permitted me between raising a family and working such jobs as counselor for the Illinois Department of Public Aid, teacher in the Chicago Public Schools, life insurance salesman, mortgage loan officer, U.S. army reservist, and, ultimately textbook editor and freelance writer.

Of these stories, two others were published in *AIM*: "The Prospect" in the Summer issue of 1982, and "Day Work" (originally published as "Swan Song") in 1985. Three of the stories in this collection, published after the release of a novel, *Reunion: A Novel of the New South*, in 1989, appeared in the 1996 collection *Guildworks: Writings by the West Side Writers Guild*. I and five other like-minded writers from that region of the city founded the association in the early '90s to encourage and promote writing about the West Side. These stories are: "A Mortgage Burning Party" and "Derelict."

It is my sincere hope that these ten stories, written over a span of twenty years do, justice to the residents of a part of Chicago whose lives have rarely if ever been immortalized in fiction, but even more, that West Siders who happen upon them come away with the affirmation that their lives were worth someone's paying attention to and chronicling for posterity.

Mark Allen Boone
Lisle, Illinois 2021

Candle in the Dark

COMED HAD THREATENED to put Old Man Cates in the dark, so he came down to the welfare office on West Madison Street to get help in paying the overdue bill. As if waiting in the long line weren't indignity enough, he had to suffer the warnings and advice of the veteran public aid recipients who flanked him in the packed lobby.

"Them goddamn utility companies ain't nothin' but crooks," Number Fourteen charged as she waited her turn to see the caseworker. "But you lookin' at a bigger crook. I ain't paid a 'lectric bill in two years and ain't going to," she vowed, nodding her head with finality.

"You won't git no help here," the old woman who drew number fifteen assured him in a know-it-all manner.

"Nothin' ever beat a try but a failure," Cates shot back, shutting her up.

At the shout of number twelve, he watched a young mother with an infant straddling her hip disappear behind a partition and heard the caseworker ask if she'd tracked down the child's father.

"She's a nosy bitch," Fourteen complained. "If she gives me a hard time, I'm gonna kick her ample ass!" she threatened.

The woman seated next to her tittered, baring teeth that were gapped like a hippo's.

"They think that just 'cause you' on welfare, you s'posed to take anything they dish out," she added in a half-whisper.

The caseworker emerged from behind the partition. Old Man Cates grinned smugly as the gap-toothed woman bolted upright, fearing her criticism had been overheard. The worker went to a bank of file cabinets nearby, opened a drawer, and removed a folder. Cates's cataract-dulled eyes followed her back to the partition entrance. Soon, through the opaque corrugated glass, he saw the young mother's figure rise. She emerged from the booth in tears. Cates clucked at the baby boy as he bounced past on his mother's hip.

"Number thirteen!" the caseworker called.

Cates sprang to his feet, his heart leaping inside his bony chest like a caged frog. Clutching the crumpled ticket in his fist, he hurried behind the screen.

The caseworker put his ticket with the preceding twelve and directed him to a chair facing her desk. She lifted a cigarette from a half-empty pack that lay on her desk, lit it, and blew a jet of smoke ceilingward.

"Did you call beforehand for an appointment?" she asked.

"No'm, I didn't," he replied. "Didn't know I had to."

"You mean you' been sittin' there all that time and didn't call beforehand for an appointment?" She was incredulous.

"No'm," he repeated guiltily.

"Why do you think we give out business cards?" she complained. "You' supposed to call before you come in. You're not the only client I've got."

"This is my first time in here, Ma'am," he explained. "I never got no business card."

He took out his wallet and removed the form letter he'd received when he was added to the rolls.

The caseworker skimmed it and returned the letter to him. Drawing on the cigarette, she flared her nostrils like an enraged bull and exhaled.

"I'll be with you in a minute," she told him, abruptly getting up to go to the files.

Old Man Cates ran his thick fingers through a clump of gray, matted hair. Between lighting her cigarette and going through the rigmarole about an appointment, the woman had wasted at least two minutes and the lobby was wall-to-wall people. Yet she had the gall to talk about how her time was so valuable.

The caseworker returned to her desk carrying a manila folder containing his case information. She lay it on her desk, took a final pull on the cigarette that had burned to a snake-like ash and mashed it out. Old Man Cates scooted closer to her desk within range of her tobacco-fouled breath.

"This is your budget, Mr. Cates," she began, working her finger down an itemized listing, reading off, in rapid-fire bursts, the allowances included in his monthly check.

What the procedure had to do with a past due electric bill, for the life of him Cates didn't know, but he indulged her anyway.

"I'm on a special diet," he broke in. "I got sugar. Don't I get no 'lowance for that?" he asked, snatching the chain that identified him as a diabetic from around his neck.

"You get a free medical card," she retorted.

"But my food," he continued. "I've got to eat special foods..."

"You get food stamps," she countered. "You're already getting the maximum," her voice climbed with impatience. "What more do you want?"

"How can I pay my 'lectric bill outta that?" he persisted, pulling the past due notice from his pocket and handing it to her. "My service could be cut off when I get home."

"You're already getting the maximum allowed," she repeated, ignoring the notice. "I can quote it to you from the manual." She reached for a vinyl binder that lay on top of a bookcase.

"Don't bother to quote me nothin'," he snapped. "I might've known I wouldn't get no consideration here."

He took the letter and bill, stuffed them into his pants pocket, and fastened the chain around his neck.

"Call for an appointment beforehand the next time you want to see me," the caseworker told him as she handed him a bus token and a white card with her name and phone number written on it. She asked him to sign a requisition for the token. As he scrawled his name, he burned to tell her that he wouldn't need to see her again, or at least hoped he'd never have to see her again, and that she needed to read a manual on how to talk to people, but he decided against it. He had to depend on her to eat.

"Number fourteen!" she called before he was out of the booth.

She'd meet her match with this one, Old Man Cates thought as the hefty woman wearing an expression that said she took no shit elbowed her way inside the small cubicle. He wished he could stick around to watch the fireworks. On the way out, he glanced at the old woman who shook her head as if a loose spring connected it to her shoulders.

"Tol' you wasn't go'n get no help here—you old enough to know you gotta take matters into your own hands."

Outside, he crossed Madison Street and waited for an eastbound bus, turning his thin body sideways to minimize exposure to the cutting wind. His bare hands searched empty pockets for warmth as he watched two boys crouch from the cold in the darkened doorway. The knife-edged wind forced him to seek refuge in a storefront himself. He was glad that the ride ahead would not be long.

When the bus arrived, Cates scurried, pigeon-toed, to the front door. The two boys ran to the rear. He dropped the token into the fare box and walked to the back of the bus, rubbing his raw hands together to warm them.

On one of the bench seats, the two boys who had sneaked on were exchanging pulls on a joint. One of them looked into Cates's face, grinned, and blew the smoke toward the littered bus floor.

"Don't you know what you just did is 'gainst the law?" Cates asked. "It's as wrong as if you stole somethin'. Furthermo', smokin' weed on the bus or anyplace else for that matter is 'gainst the law, too. But I guess y'all can't read." He pointed to the No Smoking sign posted at the back of the bus.

"We can't help it if you were stupid enough to pay, ol' man," one of them replied.

"If you want to live to be my age and git the experience I have, you've got to learn to play by the rules."

"Who wants to be as old as you?" the other boy asked. "You so old, you probably fart dust." Both broke into guffaws.

"You'll never make it to sixty-six at the rate the two of y'alls going," Cates said. "The Law'll have you frying in the chair before you reach twenty-one—mark my words," he nodded to a young female passenger who smiled, amused by the exchange.

"Drop dead old man!" one of them shouted as Cates reached for the signal cord.

The bus lurched to a halt. Empty bottles left on the floor rolled and collided with the stanchions at the suddenness of the stop.

"See you, grampaw!" they yelled before he got off the bus.

"I wouldn't have you for grandkids—neither one of you," he said before he disembarked.

He waited for the bus to pass before crossing the street. Looking into the boys jeering faces as they ridiculed him from the moving bus's window, he glared at them stonily, dug his hands into his pockets, waited for the light to change, and crossed. He could remember when the police would issue tickets for crossing against the light or crossing in the middle of the street, but that had gone by the wayside like everything else in the world had seemed to.

His apartment at Warren Boulevard near Paulina Street was two blocks from the bus stop, and he walked the distance slower than usual, pondering what course of action he'd follow concerning the delinquent electric bill.

Opening the vestibule door, he entered, his feet sliding over the urine-stained floor. Underfoot, he noticed a ripped-open envelope and picked it up. It was the disconnection notice from Commonwealth Edison warning him of the impending cut off. It had been removed from his broken mailbox. He didn't know what the culprit thought could be in the envelope—ComEd never to his knowledge had sent money along with the bills to pay them with, and he had sense enough to have the mailman slide his checks under his door when he wasn't home. Tramping up the tread-worn stairs to his second-floor apartment, he let himself in.

The two-room apartment was a firetrap. Yellowed, dated newspapers were stacked in bales on the floor in the front room. A sun-faded let-out couch was backed against a wall. On a stand in one corner of the room was a portable television set, a twisted wire coat hanger replacing the broken antenna. Above a dusty mantelpiece, tacked on the wall was a dull purple placard with the words printed in silver glitter:

JESUS IS THE LIGHT OF THE WORLD

He lay the mail on the table, not bothering to read the notice. After all, he knew he couldn't pay the bill before his check came at the end of the month anyway. As it was, he had to juggle the bills from month to month, paying one this time, the other the next, robbing Peter to pay Paul. He would call the company later and ask for an extension on the service until his check came.

Entering the kitchenette that was furnished with a card table, a folding chair, and a small stove, the once-white enamel yellowed by heat, Cates started to prepare breakfast. Standing alone in the room was an ancient icebox with the condenser on top that hummed incessantly yet, for all its noise, barely kept his insulin from spoiling.

Breakfast consisted of a cup of coffee with saccharine, a piece of toast, and oatmeal. His doctor had ordered him to eat a more balanced meal, but then the doctor wasn't buying his groceries.

"You're playing with your life, Cates," he often said.

"It's my life," Cates would reply. "Ain't got to answer to nobody for it but the Man Upstairs."

It was at his last check-up that he'd been put on bottled insulin out of fear that the pills might react to the medication he was taking for a bad heart.

Upon finishing his meal, Cates took the medicine from the icebox, and, rolling up his left sleeve, dabbed a cotton ball with alcohol to swab his arm. Jabbing the point of his syringe into the bottle's red rubber circle, he drew out thirty units. The cold needle point lying obliquely against his inner arm, he eased it under the flaccid skin and shot the cloudy liquid into his bloodstream.

Old Man Cates had had the condition for a long time, but it didn't flare up until the heart attack he'd suffered three years before. Prior to that time, he'd never been sick a day in his adult life although Irma, his late wife, had been sick enough for the both of them. Besides her frequent asthma attacks, she suffered from a crippling form of arthritis that reduced her mobility to a crawl, forcing him to carry her around the apartment. Their savings had been depleted by medical bills, the odd janitorial jobs he held during his working years didn't provide him with a pension, and he vowed he'd spend his last penny before he went on welfare, since he wasn't eligible for social security.

Irma had been dead nine years. With no children to help him, Cates knew he'd end up on some form of welfare but he hoped that his last days would be so numbered that he wouldn't have to exist on it for long.

After eating the light breakfast and taking his shot, the droning of the icebox lulled him into a doze, and he cradled his head in his arms, resting on the table, his snoring competing with the monotonous humming of the refrigerator.

❖

When he awoke half an hour later, the kitchen was still. Disoriented from the brief nap, Cates at first didn't notice the silence. Rising from the table, he wiped a wet spot from the surface and went to the front room to turn the television set on to "The Price Is Right."

The peaks of his days were in the mornings when he'd tune in to the many game shows and compete with the contestants. Many times he would beat them and would dream of winning a chance to go to Hollywood as a contestant himself. He'd seen many alert, elderly people on the show who were totally in command of their faculties, yet he knew the likelihood of his going to Hollywood was as remote as his getting enough money to manage his monthly bills. In spite of that reality, the power that filled him when he triumphed in his cramped living room was enough to sustain him in his old age—enough to reassure him of his usefulness as a member of the human race.

The set usually took a minute and a half to warm up before delivering a ghosted picture that ran every half-minute until he jarred it with the flat of his hand. When he turned the knob and waited the usual length of time, the picture failed to appear.

"Come on ol' piece of TV, damn it! What you waitin' for?"

He gave it another minute, then went behind to inspect the tubes. One of them was probably loosened from the constant jarring, he thought.

Removing the back, he found the tubes cold. He jerked the chain to the ceiling light for a closer inspection, but the bulb failed to illuminate. Cocking his ear toward the kitchen, he listened for the hum of the icebox. It finally dawned on him that the electricity had been turned off.

Gathering the notices up from the table, he read them near the light of the window. The electricity was off. It was already one day after the deadline. The notice was at least a week old. Whoever had stolen it from the mailbox must've felt guilty and returned it. What a dirty trick to pull on somebody, he thought.

After pulling himself together, Old Man Cates began searching the apartment for a candle. It would have to do until he could go to the electric company.

The next morning, he skipped his breakfast, caught a bus, and was the first customer at the office. He had to take a number like he had at the welfare office. When he was called, he took the disconnection notice to a white-haired clerk who had him sit before her desk.

"What can I do for you, Sir?" she asked.

"My lights are off, Ma'am," he replied.

"You didn't pay your bill, did you?" she asked.

"I didn't know they was goin' off," he explained. "I got that notice in the mail last week, and somebody stole it from my mailbox. When I came home from the welfare office yesterday asking for help to pay it, I found that notice on the floor. Didn't even know they was goin' to be cut off this soon."

"I can't see what anybody would want with a disconnection notice," the woman said. "Especially one that didn't belong to them. You knew the bill was past due."

"I was planning on askin' for an extension," he replied. "I won't git my check 'til the end of next week. I asked the welfare department for a little help, but the caseworker turned me down like it was coming outta her pocket."

"What do you want us to do?" the clerk asked.

"I'd appreciate it if I could git my lights on 'til I pay the bill next week—on credick," he explained. "I'll pay you next week. You got my word."

"You've been extended credit already. We bill you *after* the service has been rendered. When you pay your bill, we'll restore your service." She pressed the button on the number indicator for the next waiting customer.

"But I've been a good payin' customer all these years," Cates pleaded. "Check my record. I need my 'lectricity to keep my insulin cool in my icebox. I'm diabetic." He jerked the identification tag from around his neck and thrust it at her.

"Put the insulin near the window sill. With the weather as cold as it is, it'll keep. We can't restore the service until the bill is paid. I'm sorry. It's the rules. You'll also probably be charged a deposit since you can't pay your bill on time. It's company policy."

Old Man Cates struggled to his feet, shaking like a victim of Parkinson's disease. The words he spoke issued dryly from his throat.

"It's people like you who cause others to go against the law."

Stuffing the notice into his pocket, he stared at the woman briefly before walking out.

Outside, reeling with dizziness, Cates waited for the bus to take him home. The dizziness was because he hadn't eaten. Once he had solid food in his stomach, he'd be fine. He could function. Then he would have enough strength to make one final salvo to get his electricity restored.

The bus appeared, he climbed on and dropped the coins into the fare box, easing himself onto a seat beside a domestic who was on her way to work. As the bus jolted him closer to her with each bump, she scooted farther away from him, clutching her purse nearer.

When his stop approached, Old Man Cates pulled the signal cord, and the bus came to a violent halt, almost throwing him over a seat. He disembarked and made his doddering trek home. As he neared his building, he noticed the mailman approaching.

"How's it going, Cates?" he asked.

"It ain't goin', Roosevelt," he replied. "My 'lectric's off. I tried to git help to pay the bill but ain't had no luck."

"Make your own luck," the mailman answered. "I'd be willin' to bet you the onliest one in your building who's payin' a 'lectric bill. I know certain people who've been usin' 'lectwicity long after its been cut off. You ain't gettin' nowhere bein' a good sport."

"Day by day, I'm beginnin' to see that," Cates answered before going inside.

Later, Cates ate his breakfast slowly, mulling over his alternatives. He could live without lights but had to preserve his insulin. But then he could keep it by the windowsill like the woman at ComEd had suggested. Of course, his check would come within a few days and he'd be able to pay the bill like he'd promised. He wouldn't be stealing the service indefinitely, without paying like the woman at the welfare office. And he'd save the company the trip of having somebody come out to reconnect the meter if he did it himself. He just had to tune in to his game shows. They'd become as important to him as his insulin. The alternatives rebounded noisily in his head like billiard balls, one knocking the other out of contention until only one remained in his consciousness.

Rising from the table, he began to look for the pair of pliers that he had. Throwing on his coat, he left the apartment. The electric meters were located in the basement. He descended the stairs stealthily, although he didn't know why he feared getting caught by his neighbors.

When he reached the basement door, he drew out of his pocket a box of wooden matches. The door's lock was broken and had not been fixed. When he eased it open, a rat scurried across his foot, startling him. Holding his breath to avoid inhaling the dank basement air, he struck a match in front of a row of globed fixtures that jutted out from the wall. With weakened eyes, he followed the serrated metal disk of one of them as it slowly rotated, registering the number of kilowatts used. The match flame crept to his fingertips, and he shook it out. Striking another, he located the meter to his apartment, matching the account number on his bill with the one above the globe.

In the dark quiet of the basement, his mind began to search out justifications. He'd been fair and had played by the rules. He had asked for help but was turned down twice. The utility companies, he'd convinced himself, were only monopolies that took advantage of poor people like himself. Rich people never had to pay high bills because they had their meters read regularly. Where he lived though, they billed you what they wanted to bill you, and you had to pay or do without lights. All he'd be doing would be getting even with them for all the overcharges throughout the years. The old woman at the welfare office said he was a fool for trying to pay his bills. Maybe he was a fool, but he wouldn't be one any longer. Overcome with anger, Cates took the pliers and gripped the wire of the metal tag that locked off his electricity. With a trembling hand, he held the wire between the pliers' cold teeth. All he had to do was twist loose the tag, and his lights would be back on. It couldn't have been simpler. It was the electric company's fault for making it so easy that a child could do it yet somehow, for some reason, he couldn't force his wrist to complete the job.

Later that same evening, Old Man Cates brought out the candles that Irma used to light at Christmas. When he touched the short black wick with a match, it cast an eerie yellow glow in his dark apartment. He stared into the flame as it flickered delicately, wavering, trying to decide whether it would remain lit or snuff itself out. He watched the shadows of the objects that loomed larger than life dance on the room's walls as he moved the candle. For but a moment, he contemplated the minor miracle of how the dancing spot of fire above the wax candle provided a halo of light yet at the same time had the potential to cause a holocaust. With a strong puff of air, he blew it out, throwing the two-room apartment into total darkness before he undressed himself and wearily climbed into bed.

1974

Christmas Leave

THAT CHRISTMAS MORNING, when the M.P.s caught Jarvis Boatman dressed in long drawers and a field jacket trying to break into the Fort Dix post exchange, they handcuffed him and carried him off to the post hospital. Like everybody else in my platoon, they thought Boatman was off. I didn't believe it then and I don't believe it now that I got my walking papers in the mail. Jarvis Boatman had more sense than anybody gave him credit for having. He was playing a role that my ancestors played when they wanted to get out of a day's work: he was malingering. The difference was that Boatman faked a mental illness instead of a physical one, and it worked. After all, it got him out of the U.S. Army.

The last week we spent together as bunkmates was the week before boot camp ended. Combat commands barked in an Oklahoma drawl woke me up that Sunday morning. We were alone in the barracks and Boatman was practicing his bayonet combat technique at the other end of the room. Everybody else had left for a weekend in New York, or for a night in a motel in Wrightstown with one of the hookers that invaded the fort on payday. Me, I was saving my money for the two-week Christmas leave that was only five days away. I was so anxious to get the hell off the fort that I'd made plane reservations before our release orders were official. Boatman hadn't made his yet. He was so hung up on passing proficiency park that he never mentioned going home for Christmas like the rest of us, and it bothered me because it didn't seem normal.

I went down to the end of the barrack where Boatman was. The nearer I got to him the clearer I could hear him holler the commands: "Parry right! ... Parry left! ... Thrust! ...Withdraw! ... Recover!"

I watched him make a running lunge at the cement block wall with a broomstick and stared as he pulled his imaginary bayonet back, tracing semicircles in the air. When he caught me looking at him, he stopped.

"I'm go'n get through boot camp if it kills me," he explained. "They ain't go'n keep *me* here...

"They ain' t go'n keep nobody here," I said. "It's just a psyche job they' trying to pull on us."

Next thing I knew, Boatman threw the broom to the floor and challenged me to hand-to-hand combat. I was pretty good at it and he knew it, but he was pulling out all stops in his effort to pass.

The width between two bunks became our battleground. He crouched down, and I took the offensive immediately, lunging at him. I caught his wrist and, twisting it, brought it behind his back like a pretzel. He tried to free himself but couldn't. I brought my free arm up around his neck and forced him into a headlock. He didn't give up, though. He kept struggling and straining, trying to free himself, turning redder and redder. Finally, I lost my balance and fell to the floor, pulling him on top of me. His nose hit the edge of the bunk in the fall. Blood dropped in bright red spots on his t-shirt. Instinctively, I snatched mine off and pressed it against his nose. Leading him to the latrine, I ran cold water over the bloody shirt, wrung it out, and applied it to his nose.

"I'm sorry, man," I said. "I didn't mean to draw blood."

"It's all right," he replied. "A nosebleed never killed nobody."

"Boatman," I said. "When you go'n make reservations to go home like everybody else?

"I ain't going home," he answered from the latrine floor. The bleeding had stopped and he had braced himself against the wall, furiously rocking his torso back and forth in a series of sit-ups.

"How in the hell can you say you ain't going home?" I demanded, rinsing my hands of his blood. "It's the day we' all been looking forward to the minute we got off the bus to this fucking place," I said.

"When there's ten mouths to feed, one bein' away helps more'n it hurts," he said getting up from the floor. "I'm up to thirty sit-ups, Willie," he said.

"Bullshit!" I said. "I don't care how many mouths y'all got to feed. Your folks can't enjoy Christmas knowing you're far away from home."

"They need my money more'n they need me," he said.

He had suspended himself from the crossbar above a toilet stall, using it to do chin-ups.

"Goddammit it, Boatman! Stop!" I shouted. "Those sit-ups and chin-ups won't make a bit of difference in you passing pro park. After eight weeks you've gone from twenty-five sit-ups to thirty and you' been practicing every day including Sunday. Christmas—the time of the year everybody looks forward to, and all you can think about is staying on this fucking post. You are crazy, Boatman," I said. "Just like they all say."

Later, I sat on my bed, pulling on my socks, feeling sorry about what I'd said to Boatman. He came to sit beside me on the bunk.

"You going to church with me, Willie? We still got time to make it across the post."

"Yeah, I'll go," I said, forcing my foot through the cardboard pantleg of my starched fatigues.

The chapel was as good a place to go as any on a Sunday morning with everything else on post closed. Besides, I felt I owed it to Boatman even though I could make no sense out of a church being on a reservation that trained men for war. I just couldn't rationalize it. Boatman had convinced me to go one Sunday, saying that it would help me make it through the remaining weeks of boot camp. We had been going every Sunday ever since.

That particular Sunday, Boatman and I were the only recruits in attendance. For that reason, it seemed like the chaplain was talking directly to us. I looked over at Boatman. His eyes were closed tightly and his teeth were clenched like a kid making a birthday wish before blowing out the candles. He was praying. At that moment an idea occurred to me as though God had planted it in my head.

"Boatman," I whispered. "Why don't you go home with me for Christmas? If you don't want to go to Oklahoma, why not spend Christmas with me and my family in Chicago? It beats the hell out of staying on this post," I said.

"You' the one crazy Willie," he said. "I can't go home with you."

"My folks know you already. They just haven't *met* you."

"I never been to a big city before," he said.

"Then that's all the more reason for you to go. It'll be a change. I can't look forward to going home for Christmas knowing you go'n be stuck here. I wouldn't leave a dog on this post at this time of year," I said.

"I'm go'n be all right," he tried to assure me.

"You go'n be all right 'cause you going home with me," I told him.

It was final. He was going to Chicago for Christmas leave. I'd buy his ticket if I had to. I had a little money saved up. I had figured it all out during the church service. I'd put him up in my room while I slept on the let-out couch in the living room. I could remember my mother's old saying: Charity begins at home.

"You sure it'll be all right?" he asked as we walked back to the barracks.

"Yeah," I replied. "I won't let nobody mess with you. I know hand-to-hand combat, remember?" I took a playful swipe at him.

Back at the barracks, I gathered up the coins I'd collected to make my once-a-week call home. I decided to ask my mother because she'd understand the situation better than the old man would. I'd let *her* break the news to him. I went downstairs to the pay phone.

"Momma," I said after making the connection. "This is Willie. I need you to do me a favor. You know Boatman—my buddy, my bunkmate—the one I' been telling you about?" I asked. "Well he's not going home for Christmas, and I was wondering if I could bring him home so he won't be by himself on this post."

"Won't you ever outgrow picking up strays, Willie?" she asked. Her voice seemed farther away than the seven hundred-odd miles. "Don't he have a home to go to?"

"Yeah" I said, "but he don't want to go—he's...he's got some problems at home."

"Does *he* want to come home with you to a nigger neighborhood for two weeks, Willie? If he's crazy 'nough to come, I'm crazy 'nough to have him," she said.

"Thanks, Momma!" I said. "I knew I could count on you."

"Don't go braggin' on me until I find a way to break it to your daddy that you' bringing a white boy home for Christmas. He's go'n think both of us have lost our minds."

I ran upstairs to tell Boatman the good news. He was sitting on his footlocker spit shining his boots. He couldn't improve on the shine but true to his nature, he kept polishing the toes.

"I been thinking, Willie," he began. "What if I flunked pro park and they had to keep me here? S'pose I really started acting crazy like they say I am? What if I went to a psychiatrist, and he said: 'Boatman, you crazy.' You think they'd have to discharge me on account of me bein' unfit for military service?" He didn't look up from his boot.

"I think you'd have to really be off to dream up something like that," I said. "You could be ruined for life. Wouldn't be able to get a job or anything."

"S'pose I didn't have to get a job? S'pose I was expected to work on my folks' farm the rest of my life? Then it wouldn't make no difference, would it?"

"I guess it wouldn't matter what anybody else thought as long as you didn't have to depend on nobody for a job—and as long as you weren't really crazy."

"Yeah," he said. "You see what I'm getting at?"

"Sort of," I replied. "But it's a dangerous game. What if it backfires?"

"It's a chance I'm willing to take. I swear," he said, his blue eyes filling with tears. "They can mess with me all they want, but I ain't go'n stay here another eight weeks."

Wednesday night was a night of celebration for Delta Company. Proficiency tests had been held earlier that day and everybody in the platoon passed— everybody except Jarvis Boatman. They flunked him on drill-and-ceremony, an area that Boatman hadn't practiced very much. He had a hard time with the facing commands. Would execute a right face when the command was left face. He was nervous. Had to be. I know he knew his directions.

It was the bayonet drill that did it, though. All of us were standing in line, waiting our turn to make a running thrust at the target before us. Boatman was fourth in line and I was fifth. When the sergeant handed him the bayonet and Boatman ran to the target, he tripped. I don't know how he could have. But the rifle skittered across the ground. Boatman scraped his knuckles against the pavement and they were bleeding. Everybody in the platoon laughed but me. I felt for Boatman.

Afterwards, when he found out that he'd flunked and would have to repeat boot camp with the winter cycle of recruits, Boatman couldn't face me. He went off to be by himself. I understood that he needed time alone. But I didn't want to spend another night in the same barracks with the other trainees either.

I lay on the bottom bunk, writing the last letter I expected to write from Fort Dix. I wanted it to reach Chicago before Boatman and I arrived that Friday on the seven-thirty flight. In the letter, I asked my folks to be extra kind to him since Boatman had flunked pro park. I was glad that he was going home with me because he needed a lift in spirits. Finishing the letter, I stamped it and got up to go to the mailbox. As I was leaving the bay, I heard a voice from the other end of the barracks shout, "Let's fuck up Boatman's bunk! He blew our perfect record!"

"Yeah!" another voice agreed.

I didn't know what they meant until I saw cans of beer sail across the barracks, crashing against the floor. I guessed they were going to soak his mattress with the leftover cans of beer.

In the hall I listened as someone said, "Yeah, that's right, do it at the foot of his bed—no, under that shit-head's pillow!" Then I heard whistles and hoots of laughter, followed by a grunting sound, and I knew what was happening. Somebody was relieving himself on Boatman's bed. Afterwards, they all ran out of the barracks, whooping with laughter. Randy Carter brought up the rear, pulling up his drawers.

The fact that Boatman and I were bunkmates didn't matter. Neither did it matter that I was there. I didn't count. Maybe I should've been glad that they didn't shit in my bed. I didn't want Boatman to know that a person could stoop so low as to shit in a place where another rested his head so I dislodged the shit into a fold of the sheet, took it to the latrine, and flushed it down the toilet. I went back and turned Boatman's mattress over, took a sheet from an empty bunk and put it on his. I wouldn't tell him what they had done. I wouldn't've wanted anybody to tell me if it had happened to me.

Jarvis Boatman didn't return to the barracks that night, and I didn't see him that Thursday either. When Friday came, I got worried. I asked all over the post about his whereabouts but nobody knew where he was. As I folded up my clothes and packed them in the duffel bag, preparing for the two-week leave, I wondered where he could have gone.

Desperate, I locked up my belongings and went to the company headquarters to find out if they'd heard anything, but they hadn't. With a vague idea of where he might be, I set out for the post chapel where we attended services on Sundays, hoping that the chaplain had heard from him.

By then, I was getting more mad than worried about Boatman. He knew I'd made plans to take him home with me for Christmas. If he'd backed out at the last minute, why the hell couldn't he be man enough to tell me? Why disappear without telling the one person who'd been closest to him those eight weeks? It wasn't right.

When I reached the chapel, I burst through the doors and ran straight to the chaplain's study but it was empty. Little light filtered through the stained-glass windows, and the sanctuary was almost dark. On my way down the aisle, I spotted a form crouched on the floor between the last two pews.

"Boatman!" I yelled. "Jarvis Boatman!" I hollered, running over to him. "Man, I've been worried about you. Why didn't you let me know where you were?"

"I had to be by myself," he replied. "Didn't want nobody to know where I was. I knew that the church, on a weekday, was the last place anybody'd come."

"You' still going to Chicago with me, ain't you, Boatman?" I asked.

He didn't answer. He looked at me as though he could see straight through me. His three-day-old beard made him look like a hobo. The uniform he had on hadn't been changed in three days.

"Ain't you going with me to pack?" I asked. "We' got a flight leaving at seven-thirty tonight. I got the money for both of our tickets. You don't have to worry about paying me back."

"I ain't going with you, Willie," he said.

"What in the hell do you mean?" I yelled. "I made plans and my folks are expecting you and now you tell me at the last minute you ain't coming? What's the matter with you, Boatman?" I asked.

"I'm going home, Willie," he replied. "I'm going back to Oklahoma where I belong"

"You what?" I asked dumfounded.

"I'm going home," he repeated. "H-O-M-E."

"You going home?" I asked, shaking his shoulders, and laughing, almost to the point of tears. "You mean my preaching finally got to you? Hell, I don't really give a damn about you not going to Chicago, as long as you' going home for Christmas. That's all that really counts. Now I don't have to carry it on my conscience that I left you spending the holidays at this godforsaken place. But where've you been these last few days?" I asked. "I' been looking everywhere for you. You been here all along?"

"Yeah, I been here, Willie," he said. "Asking why the Lord chose me to be recycled when I tried harder than anybody else in the platoon. But you know what He told me, Willie? He said, Jarvis, I been working through you. I been using you as an instrument and now I don't need you here no more, so I'm sending you back home to Oklahoma." He had a wild gleam in his eyes that scared me.

I was trying to make sense out of what he was telling me, but I had

23

trouble. Spending two nights in a chapel, talking directly to God and, what was worse, God answering him—in complete sentences. It was all so weird.

"He said I had to explain why I ain't goin' to Chicago with you, Willie. You see, I got my own cross to bear and you can't help me bear it. Christ had His own cross to bear and nobody helped Him."

I guess if I'd heard those words coming from somebody else I could've accepted them more easily, but they were hard for me to take coming from Boatman. He said them so calmly that it was as though his spirit had been taken over by somebody else.

"I started to write you a note and tell you I was goin' home, but He said for me to tell you to your face. I was just getting ready to go over to the barracks to talk to you before you came. He must've sent you here to save me the trouble."

"I guess so," I said.

"Well, we better get on back. After all, we gotta pack," Boatman said.

On the way back to the barracks, Boatman walked stiffly, like a programmed soldier who didn't know when to drop the military march for a natural stride. We hardly talked on the way back.

I didn't see him again until after Christmas leave. I had to return to Fort Dix for my advanced training and I would be there for another two months, only my new assignment was at the opposite end of the fort.

The day I reported to my new duty station, I ran into one of the trainees who had been in Boatman's and my platoon.

"You heard about Boatman?" he asked.

"No, what about him?" I replied.

"He went off the deep end. Took leave of his senses. The M.P.s caught him trying to break into the PX the week after we left for Christmas leave. All he had on was long drawers, a field jacket, and a pair of boots."

"Where's he now?" I wanted to know. "They send him home?"

"I heard he's still in the army hospital. Hear they go'n discharge him on account of him bein' off his rocker."

I flagged down a post taxicab to take me to the hospital. When I got there, the doctor tried to stop me from seeing Boatman. Said Boatman wouldn't recognize me and that visitors wouldn't do him any good. Said Boatman didn't even answer to his own name.

When I entered the ward, I saw him lying flat on his back wearing a striped hospital gown. A sheet was stretched to his throat and his listless eyeballs were fixed on the ceiling. One wrist was shackled to the bedpost and his face was as white as the sheet that covered him.

"Boatman!" I called out.

His eyes didn't move. I pulled a chair over to his bed and drew the curtain around us.

"How you feeling?" I asked. "This is Willie Bowles, your friend."

He didn't answer.

"Look man," I whispered, "I know you putting on an act, but give me some sign that you understand me. I won't let the cat out the bag. We friends, remember?"

He still didn't answer, but water formed at the corners of his eyes.

"Boatman, I thought you were going home," I said. "You told me you were going home for Christmas, Jarvis," I said, trying to make him remember.

"I am going home," he said.

He was all right, I told myself. He had answered in a logical sentence. It was like the straight line on a heart monitor all of a sudden shot upward.

"What were you doing at the PX?" I asked.

"I was doing my Christmas shopping," he replied, a trace of humor in his voice.

"But you weren't even dressed, and the PX was closed."

"He told me to go and find some clothes to go home in. I did what he told me to."

"Who?" I asked.

"The Lord Jesus Christ," Boatman replied.

I lowered my voice to a whisper.

"I'm on to you, Boatman. You can't fool me. You' jiving me and I know it. I remember how you asked me if a person who acted crazy could get out on a general discharge. You said you had nothing to lose 'cause you were expected to work on the family farm anyway." I shook his shoulders to get him to respond.

"But why did you join the army in the first place?" I continued. "They didn't draft you. You didn't have to join."

He smiled.

"God sent me here, I told you."

"You don't have to talk, Boatman. Not if you don't want to," I said. "I know the real truth. I know you ain't crazy. You smart. Real smart. It takes a lot of brains to come up with a scheme like this."

"You can't bear my cross for me, and I can't bear your cross for you. Christ carried His own cross. Every man's gotta carry his own," Boatman said, repeating the same words he'd said before Christmas.

The nurse said it was one of the few things he'd said since the M.P.s had picked him up. She shook her head sadly. I knew what she was thinking.

"He's not crazy," I told her. "He's got more sense than everybody thinks."

But she looked at me as if I were talking out of my head, as if I belonged in a bed right next to Boatman with my wrist shackled to the bedpost.

I wanted to tell her just how smart Boatman was—that he was faking— that he was making an ass out of her, the doctor, the M.P.s, and the whole United States Army.

As I walked down the hospital corridor, thinking about what Boatman had said, I began to understand what he had been telling me all along. He wasn't crazy. I was positive of it. We choose to believe what we want to believe, and

I chose to believe that Boatman had been sent on a mission—a mission that he might not have understood fully, but a mission just the same.

The hospital chapel was ahead of me and as I entered, I fell to my knees and prayed as hard as I had in my whole life. I prayed for Jarvis Boatman. I prayed that he wasn't as crazy as everybody thought he was; but that if he was crazy, he was crazy like a fox.

1975

A Qualified Prospect

SUMMER HAD COME EARLY, and Wayne Russell's shirt clung like cellophane to his back, but his manager drove with the windows of the Mercedes Benz closed to give the impression that the air conditioner was working. Through the windshield, Wayne looked at his old neighborhood's unemployed, driven from their apartments by the unseasonable heat, hanging out on stoops, on porches, and at the curbsides, their sweating faces glistening in the hot sun.

"Look at 'em!" Augustus Reed complained as the car approached Wayne's old neighborhood. "Wouldn't recognize a job if one bit 'em."

Wayne didn't reply. The idle bodies reminded him of his agency manager's Monday morning dictum: "When you sell life insurance, you wake up every morning unemployed." For Wayne, the truth of the statement hit home and he suddenly felt like one of them.

He picked up the open appointment book that lay on the seat next to him and looked at the near empty page. *Thursday, June fifth.* One sales appointment for the entire day. *Prospect's name:* Horace Lee. He closed the book.

Three nights before, he had spent two hours on the telephone trying to get sales interviews for the coming work week. Reed required Wayne and the other five agents in his charge to schedule no fewer than fifteen appointments per week, but Wayne's list of friends, acquaintances, and former job associates ran out in less than a month. And when, in desperation, he called some of the many "Russells" listed in the Chicago phone book hoping that their having a common name would result in an appointment, he was hung up on before he could deliver the sales pitch. Rather than pick names at random out of the phone book (which other agents had turned to), Wayne decided that he'd have better odds in trying to educate his old neighbors about the wonders of "income replacement." The summer sales campaign for *Greater Security Insurance* had just started. Augustus Reed, whose own fortunes as a manager were riding on the success of his new recruits, accompanied Wayne to close the sale.

Although he had grown up in the neighborhood, Wayne had lost contact with the people. He had survived the gang warfare, alcoholism, and drug addiction that were rife and managed to put himself through college, majoring in social work with the intention of helping to better the conditions he was able to rise above. The fact that he had risen above them contributed to his failure: he was seen as a member of the establishment that these people blamed for their condition. Shortly after he left the field, burnt out, cynical and with no job prospects, Wayne was introduced to Reed by a mutual friend who had entered the business and had sold a million dollars of insurance in his first year.

In Reed's eyes, Wayne had the people experience that being a good insurance salesman required. Never mind the lack of sales skills. Reed assured him that those could be taught. But what couldn't be taught was how to deal with people. A person could have all the sales skills in the world; you could know your product backward and forward, but if you didn't know how to deal with people, you couldn't make it in the business. Wayne had half the battle won, Reed insisted. He had the makings of a top producer. Wayne didn't resist the pitch. After all, he was in desperate need of a job.

He had written Horace Lee down as a "suspect" when he first compiled his monthly list of prospects. Later, after Wayne had heard from a reliable source that Horace had gotten a good-paying job, Horace became, in insurance lingo, "a qualified prospect," a plum ripe for the picking.

Augustus Reed parked the car. Fifteen minutes early for the appointment, he rehearsed with Wayne the strategy to get Horace to buy.

"OK, what're you gonna do first?" Reed asked.

"I'll ask him what his ideas about life insurance are," Wayne answered. "In order to get a feel for where he's at."

"Then what?" Reed went on. He grinned, his capped teeth as perfect as piano keys.

"I'll ask him how much insurance he has already," Wayne replied.

"Go on. What did I train you to say next?" Reed inquired, urging him on like a coach trying to get the most out of a prized player.

"I'll ask him just how much he thinks a man in his situation ought to have. After that, I'll tell him how much he *should* have as head of a family of four according to this article by the *Wall Street Journal*." Wayne pulled out an article on which he'd underscored in red ink the title, "How Much Insurance Do You Need?"

"You've got it Wayne!"

Reed threw back his head and crowed a laugh at the roof of the car.

"Sell him that hundred thousand dollar policy! Let me add up my production points."

He took out a pocket calculator, poking at the buttons with his fingertips.

"You' go'n make me manager of the year!" he exclaimed.

Wayne wiped his forehead and turned on the radio to hear the weather report. A newscaster announced the latest unemployment statistics. Wayne snapped the radio off. Pulling out his handkerchief, he soaked up the sweat from his face and neck. Both got out of the car.

"Hey Wayne! Wayne Russell!" a voice rang out from several feet away. Wayne looked in its direction.

"It's me! Riley Mills!" a young man yelled, flanked by two other idlers. Wayne had gone to high school with Riley.

Impatiently, Reed checked his watch as Wayne walked over to speak. He introduced Reed to Wilson, Reed standing apart from the group as if they were a spectacle in the center of a circus ring.

"What you doing in the 'hood, Wayne?" Riley asked. "Thought you had wrote us off!"

"I've got an insurance appointment with Horace Lee," Wayne replied.

"Yeah, and we're gonna be late," Reed interjected, looking at his watch.

"Lee ain't go'n buy a dime's worth of insurance from you," Riley said. "Velucci's got this territory sewed up. Nobody buys no insurance lessen it's from him."

"That may be," Reed butted in. "But Wayne sells the kind of insurance few black folks have been exposed to. Veluccci's company probably doesn't even carry it."

Riley Mills gave him a look as if to say, "Muthafucka I didn't pull your chain."

"Later Riley," Wayne said, defusing the tension between the two. "I'm running late for the appointment."

He knew that it was of no use trying to explain the ins and outs of income replacement to somebody who had no income to replace, so Wayne didn't bother to try.

As he and Reed entered the hallway of Horace's apartment building, Wayne was hit with the odors his memory had buried. Aromas from boiling pots and frying skillets collided in the air, competing for dominance.

When the two of them reached Horace's door, Wayne sat down his attaché case, ran his palms over his lapels, and tightened his tie. He knocked on the door.

The delay in answering made him uneasy. With his luck, Horace probably wasn't even home. In the insurance business, Wayne had been stood up too often to think about, and the thing about it was that the people didn't feel the least bit guilty when you called them later to find out why.

He checked his watch. He was only three minutes late. The look of annoyance on Reed's face made Wayne feel guilty for even having accepted the appointment.

"You've got to upgrade your clientele," Reed said. "You've got to get some upscale clients. That was my mistake in starting out. I wasted too much time on black folks—*poor* black folks."

The door opened. Horace loomed over them, bare-chested, the tight black hair drawn closer to his chest because of the heat. He wiped his red eyes with the back of his hand.

"Damn near forget you was coming," he said, stifling a yawn. "Come on in, Wayne. Have a seat in the living room. I'll be out as soon as I get some clothes on." He went into a bedroom.

Wayne, at Reed's prompting, went into Horace's kitchen. He moved everything on the table to one side and pulled up a chair. One of the rules of the business was that the salesman controlled the interview, which meant even setting the atmosphere. If a television set was going, Wayne would politely tell the potential client to turn it off. If the prospect's wife was in the kitchen washing dishes, he would invite her into the conversation. A wife could be a valuable ally in getting a stubborn prospect to buy. All of this Reed had taught him in the first week in the business.

The two of them sat at the table with Wayne's open briefcase. Wayne was holding a rate book in his hand when Horace entered.

"I guess the kitchen is as good a place as any," he said, somewhat disarmed by Wayne's initiative.

"In my experience I've found it to be," Reed responded, introducing himself with a handshake.

"Let me tell you up front that I'm not buying nothing today, Wayne," Horace cautioned him. "I told you could come over on account of me knowing your family for so long."

"When I called for the appointment, I said that I had some ideas to share with you about life insurance," Wayne said. "That's all I plan to do. Of course, if you put a gun to my head forcing me to sell you a policy, I won't argue." Both Horace and Augustus Reed laughed.

Wayne had grown tired of being told that the prospect wasn't going to buy. He knew that nobody ever bought anything unless a need was uncovered. Augustus Reed had taught him that. It was Wayne's job to uncover the need.

Reed sat still, seemingly detached, disinterested, although Wayne knew that he'd be ready to jump in the minute the potential sale fell into danger.

"Tell me what you think about life insurance, Horace," Wayne asked, his hands clasped.

"I think it's a good thing," Horace replied. "After all, everybody's go'n die someday, and it costs money to die just like its costs money to live."

Reed dropped his head and picked at his teeth with a business card. Wayne could read his mind: Nigger you don't know *how* to live.

"The trouble with our people is that they can't see ahead of the grave when it comes to insurance," Wayne began. "The only insurance we know about is burial insurance. If we put the money we waste on nickel and dime policies with a company like *Greater Security*, we'd get more in the long run. Did you know there are *living* benefits to life insurance?" Wayne asked.

"What you mean by living benefits?" Horace asked skeptically. "How can there be living benefits when the one who bought the policy is dead? He ain't getting no benefits out of a piece of paper."

Reed rolled his eyes toward the ceiling.

"What I mean," Wayne said, "is that the insured can take advantage of the policy when he's alive. You've got kids don't you Horace?"

"Yeah, I got two... twelve and five."

34

"You want them to have it better in life than you've had it don't you, Horace?"

"Tell me who wouldn't," Horace responded.

"Then you understand the importance of a college education in today's world," Wayne said. *"Greater Security has plans that can pay for your children's education. That's one of the many living benefits that insurance can offer."*

Wayne looked into Reed's eyes, searching for a sign of approval. Horace scooted his chair closer to the table where Wayne had lain a pre-printed worksheet with the details of a hundred-thousand-dollar insurance plan for a male aged thirty-four. He had abandoned his earlier strategy, having hit Horace's "hot button" with the question on education, and was hell-bent on pursuing it until a sale resulted.

"Let me show you how much cash accumulates in this plan after six years—the time when your oldest will be ready for college," Wayne offered.

He then went on to explain, column by column, how the cash value increased year after year and how, together with the dividends the company paid, the policy would yield a reasonable sum—enough to pay the first year's college tuition. Horace's eyes were fixed on the dollar figure as Wayne explained the plan.

"Almost like a bank account ain't it?" Horace asked.

Reed's eyes twinkled with the prospect of a sale.

"Yeah," Wayne replied. "Only with this plan, you get that much if you live but your family gets one hundred thousand dollars when you die. Tell me about a bank account that pays your family that much when you die," Wayne challenged him.

"How much is it go'n cost me? I know you don't get something for nothing," Horace replied.

"How much can you afford to pay?" Wayne countered, knowing that he'd lose Horace if he quoted too high a premium. "What we do at *Greater Security* is to determine how much a person can afford to pay comfortably, and then we tailor a plan to fit his needs. You like steak, don't you?" he asked.

"Yeah," Horace responded. "Who don't?"

"Then you wouldn't take a porterhouse and stuff it down your throat all at once, would you?"

Wayne could feel Horace biting. He saw it in his eyes. He couldn't blow it, though. It was why he had thrown the ball back into his court to let Horace decide how much he could afford.

"You couldn't enjoy it—you'd choke," Horace answered.

Reed laughed, beaming with approval. Wayne could see that he was impressed by the way in which he had absorbed everything that had been taught him, even down to the analogy about the steak.

"That's the point," Wayne said. "You'd cut it up into nice, bite-sized pieces—chunks that you could swallow easily without getting choked. The same way you buy life insurance. You buy what the budget can handle and then you build gradually on the program year by year as you can afford to. I promise to sit down with you and evaluate your insurance plan every year, and, where necessary, suggest changes."

Wayne had taken out an application form and his gold Cross pen. On a legal pad he drew an arrow. At one end point, he wrote in a zero. At the other end, he wrote in the dollar cost of the program he proposed for Horace.

"You're somewhere between zero and this figure," he told Horace. "It's up to you to tell me where you are. You have to tell me how much you can comfortably afford."

Horace thought a few seconds and answered.

"Fifty dollars a month."

While it wasn't quite what Wayne had hoped, it was still a reasonable premium and would generate several production points. With a couple more sales like it, he could easily meet his monthly sales quota. The nagging doubts about staying in the business had left him temporarily.

"Do you use a middle initial?" he asked Horace as he began to fill out the application.

"M," Horace replied.

Augustus Reed looked eager, like a hungry dog waiting for a feeding.

Before Wayne could ask for Horace's social security number, he heard a loud knock on the front door.

"If you ignore it, maybe the person'll go away," Wayne wanted to say, but didn't.

Horace got up.

"I'll be back in a minute," he said.

Wayne filled out what he could without Horace's help. He heard the door shut followed by Horace and another man's voice. Entering the kitchen with Horace was a man dressed in a Hawaiian print sport shirt and black slacks. Around his right wrist he wore a gold bracelet, and on his left, a Rolex. He appeared to be the same age as Wayne. Horace introduced him as Jack Velucci.

"I don't want you to think I don't trust you, Wayne," Horace said, "but I've been dealing with Jack for so long that I wanted his advice on the policy you' writing for me."

"You mean the policy Wayne *was* writing for you," Reed said, ripping the application in two. He slammed Wayne's attaché case shut. "Let's go!," he said. "We don't have to put up with this shit. It's not ethical."

Velucci took Wayne by the arm, and Wayne looked into his blue eyes— eyes that looked like they had seen all and had been hardened by what they had taken in.

"I want to tell you why Horace is so loyal," he said.

"I'd rather know why he's so *disloyal* to his own," Reed demanded.

"I don't know about Wayne, but you sure as hell ain't one of his own," Velucci retorted.

Reed stalked out, slamming the door, but Wayne remained behind.

"I'm more than the insurance man to them," Velucci explained. "When they get letters from the government or complicated forms to fill out, I'm the one they ask for help. When some of 'em need a few dollars to tide 'em over until their check comes, I'm the one they can call with no questions asked. They pay me back...better than my own that I lend money to. I can come into this neighborhood any time of day or night and feel safe and welcome. The biggest compliment they can pay me is to ask my advice about a policy my competition is trying to sell. I wouldn't trade this route for nothing."

Wayne couldn't think of anything to say. He went to the door.

"I'm sorry, Wayne," Horace said. "Guess things have changed around here since you left."

"Yeah, I guess they have," Wayne replied, shaking Horace's hand.

When he stepped back out into the hot sun, Wayne heard his name. It was Riley Mills again.

"You sell Horace?"

Wayne shook his head no.

"Told you!" Riley yelled, hooting and high-fiving the open palms of his cohorts.

Wayne approached Reed's car. On its rear bumper was a sticker that read: *"Your Life Is My Life's Work."*

Wayne read the sign, thinking that there were a number of other things to devote his life to. With no other interviews scheduled, he would have to ride with Reed, possibly making cold calls—"gold calls" Reed called them— knocking on business doors trying to sell employee group insurance plans. It was too hot for it, Wayne thought. Furthermore, if he were on the other side of the door, he'd turn down any sweaty, fast-talking salesman who called on him and would feel justified in doing it.

Reed rolled down the window.

"You might as well go with me to pound the pavement, knocking on doors. You'll learn yet to stay away from poor folks—poor *black* folks," he cautioned.

Wayne did not get in.

"I'm going back to the office to get my things," he said. "You'll have to go without me."

"What the fuck do you mean?" Reed asked. "If you can't come with me, you can keep on walking."

Wayne loosened his tie and collar and removed his sports jacket, and walked toward the bus stop. Reed called him, but Wayne kept walking. Reed sped off with the windows still rolled up.

Wayne thought that any Mercedes he would drive would be new, not used, and the air conditioner would be working on the hottest day of the year. As he walked to the bus stop, Wayne passed a jobless teenager who held a boom box that blasted out the lazy lyrics of "Hot Fun in the Summertime." When it ended, the same reporter whom Wayne had heard earlier announce the unemployment figures, gave the weather forecast. Rain was predicted for later in the afternoon—heavy thundershowers.

The year that Wayne had been in the insurance business he had developed an odd appreciation for the rain that fell on days when he had no scheduled appointments. Rain washed away the guilt he felt for not walking the streets on perfect sunny days, peddling insurance for *Greater Security*. Rain was the perfect excuse for not pounding the pavement in a downpour, trying to sell what the zealots called "the greatest product ever conceived by the mind of man."

As he waited for the bus, now an unemployment statistic himself, Wayne felt a sense of relief. Better to be an official statistic than somebody who deludes himself into thinking he is a contributing member of the work force when he was not, or, even worse, somebody who had gotten where he was at the expense of people he considered to be beneath him. He had to sustain this sense of self-esteem for the job of selling himself to an employer. But he was up to the job. If he could sell an idea—something that a person couldn't see, touch, taste, or smell, he could sell anything, including himself. His savings would take him through the summer and about the fall he wasn't worried. After all, he could always teach.

1978

A Citizen's Protest

WITH THE ONE GOOD EYE left in his head, Fullman Smith watched, from his apartment window, his nine-year-old granddaughter being pursued by a stray dog. The child ran for cover toward a parked late-model Buick and scrambled for the hood, the slick soles of her patent leather shoes slipping against the car's finish.

Fullman realized that if he'd let her wear her gym shoes like she'd begged him to earlier, that while she might not have outrun the dog, her shoes would have given her at least enough traction to climb safely onto the car's hood. But it was fall and he refused to have Penny wearing gym shoes year-round like the other neglected kids on the block.

As he watched the incident, his first mind told him to get his gun and shoot the dog dead in its tracks as it escaped with Penny's lunch, but his better judgment told him that that wasn't the civilized way to handle the situation. Besides, from his third floor window he might not've been such a good shot—especially with a moving target.

When Penny ran hysterically upstairs, he first checked to make sure that the dog's teeth hadn't broken any skin, and satisfied that they hadn't, kept her in for the day and called out the city's dogcatchers.

There was no special reason for him to think they'd come out this time after his having complained to the City of Chicago every day that week that Maypole Street wasn't safe for anyone on two legs, but Fullman gave it another try to show that he had at least attempted to go through the proper channels.

When the third day came and went without any action from the city, he decided that he had cause to organize a citizen's protest, and, after escorting Penny to school that morning, he went to the corner drug store and bought a large white cardboard poster and a black felt-tipped marker.

He hunched over the small table in his kitchen and carefully positioned the placard. Gripping the marker, he guided the tip across the surface, his hand coming to rest after the exclamation point. For extra emphasis, he enlarged it. Propping the sign against the wall, he backed away to get the perspective the remaining eye would give him.

RID MAYPOLE STREET OF DOGS NOW!

The words were a little off-center, but he judged the sign good enough to serve its purpose. What he needed now was a sturdy stick to attach it to and a loyal following to rally behind it. The former he was certain to find among the trash that littered his building's backyard; the latter he'd have to round up through some serious door-knocking.

On the way out of his apartment, he'd stop at Bobbie Hale's apartment and ask her to sign a blank petition that he'd saved from an unsuccessful attempt to oust their current alderman. At the top of the petition where the words "Nominating Petition" had been, he had crossed them out and wrote: Petition to Rid Maypole Street of Dogs.

Sign in hand, he locked his door, stretching the burglar gate across the entrance. Although he wasn't leaving the neighborhood, he wasn't taking the chance of having his apartment broken into.

When he knocked on Bobbie's door, the strident barking of her terrier unsettled him more than usual. He thought about the barking the strays did when they gathered at the empty lot across the street.

She undid the bolts that safely locked her in from the real world, put the night chain on, and cracked her door.

"Mornin' Bobbie," Fullman greeted her. "You got the privilege of being the first one to sign my petition against the dogs." He extended the pen and paper to her.

"What dogs?" she asked.

She probably wasn't even aware of the problem, Fullman thought, since she only left her apartment to take the garbage out or to babysit for Lona Mason, who lived on the first floor. He slipped the sign through the opening for her to read.

Bobbie read the words haltingly, each seeming to represent an insurmountable obstacle. When she finished, she slipped the sign through the crack and threw the pen at him.

"I ain't signing nothin' about riddin' no neighborhood of dogs!" she loud-talked him. "I'd look like a damn fool when I got a dog myself."

"I'm not talkin' about your dog. I'm talkin' about loose dogs—riddin' the streets of stray dogs," Fullman explained, taken aback.

But Bobbie didn't wait for the explanation. Slammed the door and locked it.

"I ain't signing a goddamned thing!" she shouted from the other side.

"Anybody with common sense would know I wasn't talkin' about a licensed dog," Fullman muttered.

He picked the pen up. Reaching into his pocket, he took out the marker and inserted a caret between the words *of* and *dogs* and wrote in the word *stray*. Next, he went down to Joe Pincham's apartment to seek his support.

"Hi Pinch," he greeted the old man, who opened the door slowly.

A mole the size of a small pea protruded from the edge of his left nostril. Fullman had seen curious children try to pick it off of Pinch's nose.

"I'm circulatin' this petition to git rid of the stray dogs on Maypole Street, and I need all the support I can get."

Pinch invited him in.

"Knocked on Bobbie's door and she figured I was includin' her dog," Fullman said.

"Her'n that dog's so close I'd bet money he's mor'n a pet to her," Pinch laughed. "What's the sign say?"

"It says *Rid Maypole Street of Stray Dogs Now!*," Fullman read the words. "I need as many signatures I can get to take my protest downtown. Penny was bit on her way to school the other morning."

"I ain't got my glasses," Pinch said. "I can't sign nothin' without my glasses."

"Do the best you can," Fullman persisted. "I'm countin' on you."

He had never seen Pinch with glasses in the seven years he'd known him. He figured it was an excuse to get out of signing the petition.

"How's that grandgal of yours anyhow?" Pinch inquired as he pretended to look for his glasses in another room. "You got a lot of patience trying to raise her yourself."

"She's doin' just fine—sharp as a tack in school," Fullman replied.

Joe Pincham spent ten minutes looking for the glasses but came out empty-handed.

"Can't find 'em, Full," he said. "I'm sorry."

"I'm batting a thousand already," Fullman said, leaving the apartment.

Before he asked for another signature, he debated whether or not he should drop the idea. Who else in the neighborhood would be sympathetic to his cause if he couldn't even get a hundred percent support from his own building? Where was his credibility? Here he was, half blind and advancing

44

in age, practically fumbling in the dark trying to correct a problem that nobody with two good eyes had made an effort to do something about. But he had to do something, he thought. To refuse to act was to admit defeat.

Lona Mason's was the next apartment he'd pass before going out to get a staff for his sign. She'd support him for sure. After all, she had four kids and three of them attended the same school as Penny. They had to pass the vacant lot where the strays collected just like Penny had to, and there was no other route to school without their going blocks out of the way. On second thought though, Fullman believed Lona would take the easy way out. She'd keep the children out of school. Still, he thought it was well worth a try. Maybe she'd surprise him.

He knocked on her door. When she opened it, he handed her the pen and petition. She read the words aloud.

"Will you sign it Lona?" he asked. "I'm trying to make the streets safe for the kids."

She studied the petition as if there was fine print that she couldn't understand.

"I can't sign it," she said finally.

"Why not?" Fullman asked.

"I'm on Aid and I might get cut off if they find out I signed my name," she said. She closed her door.

Fullman shook his head. Twenty-four years old with a house full of kids, no husband and no prospect of one and she couldn't sign a piece of paper that tried to guarantee her own children's safety. *If she represented the future, just what was the world coming to?* he asked himself.

"It's going to the dogs," he answered his own question.

The apathy was the very thing that he was fighting to keep from affecting Penny. His own daughter—Penny's mother—had run off when Penny was two, leaving her with him and claiming that she'd be back when she got her

45

head together. Fullman hadn't heard from her since. He figured she'd never gotten her head together. But it was just like her mother had done twelve years before, complaining that she was tired of his one-man crusades—tired of him trying to change situations that were as fateful as badly dealt hands of cards. To this day Fullman didn't know where either of them was—whether they were dead or alive. Maybe they'd met up with each other, after all, they thought alike—were cloth cut from the same bolt.

But Penny was the seed of change. If he could see to it that she broke the chain that her grandmother had started, then his life would have counted for something. If he could show Penny that a person can have an effect on changing his lot for the better he'd be grateful.

The Department of Children and Family Services didn't approve of his raising Penny after her mother ran off. They said that not only was he too old, but that he was "materially and emotionally incapable of providing the sensitive care that a girl like Penny required." So they placed her in foster home after foster home but she always found a way to return to him.

He fought the department, enlisting the aid of the local media, arguing that, in order for Penny to survive in what was becoming a cold, uncivilized world, she needed the firm guidance of a person who'd learned to cope in it.

When the media got hold of the story, the tide turned in his favor. A reporter interviewed him at length on live television, providing him with the forum to explain why it meant so much to him to raise the only grandchild he had. He recalled the cameras fixed on him and Penny as he combed her hair during the interview in a media-inspired attempt to prove that he could groom her properly.

Letters of support and money poured in from all over the city and state championing a grandfather's right to raise his own granddaughter. When the courts finally ruled in his favor, Fullman vowed publicly that, as long as he was her guardian, he'd see to it that Penny would enjoy the best care he could provide.

It occurred to him that if the papers and television could get behind him to help him win one fight—a fight involving the custody of his grandchild, that they could also support him in a battle against the environment that threatened her wholesome upbringing. That in mind, Fullman Smith returned to his apartment.

He pulled out the local telephone directory and began flipping the pages. When he found the listing for TV stations, he ran his finger down the page until he found the one that aired his and Penny's story.

Finding a pencil nearby, he wrote the number on a slip of paper, went to the phone and dialed. When the operator answered with the station's call letters, he asked her to connect him with the reporter who had directed the spot on his custody battle to get Penny.

When he learned that she was no longer with the station, he demanded to speak to the news director.

"I'm the one that y'all did a special on seven years ago about the grandfather fighting to get custody of his granddaughter Penny," he explained. "Y'all even came to my house to interview us. Let me speak to the director. He'll remember me."

The operator switched him to the director and he explained who he was and how the station had helped him before.

"I need your help again," he said. "Our neighborhood's turned into a jungle. Stray dogs are takin' over. Maypole ain't safe to walk no more."

"Did you call animal control?" the director asked.

"Called 'em a number of times," Fullman explained, "but I figure they either scared, or they don't care since we don't live on the Gold Coast. If you could put it on the news, where the city could see it for itself, maybe we'd get some help."

When the manager told him that the story wasn't newsworthy—that it wasn't important enough to dispatch a camera to the scene, Fullman got angry.

"It'd be newsworthy if it was your neighborhood, wouldn't it?" he asked.

The director told him that they had more serious issues to devote air time to.

"Bring your cameras down to the twenty-five hundred block of Maypole tomorrow morning at eight o'clock," Fullman said before hanging up. "I'll have something newsworthy for you. I guarantee it."

A short while later, he descended the stairs to the backyard. Stepping over broken bottles, rocks, and garbage, he scavenged for a suitable stick to use for his sign. When he found one, he headed back upstairs.

On the way up, he passed Bobbie on the stairs, making her trip to the garbage can. Her dog was off the leash and when she saw Fullman, she dropped the bag on the landing, spilling the contents. Snatching up the dog and holding him close to her, she trained her sharp eyes on Fullman like two hard, black pieces of coal.

"He ain't go'n hurt you Sparky. Not while I'm here," she said, looking Fullman in the eye.

"No, Bobbie, I ain't go'n hurt him, not as long as you keep him on a leash and off the street." He tucked the sign under his arm.

"You dead-eyed bastard," she said. "You might just be needing a dog to lead you around someday."

Her words stung him to the core. He'd given her no reason to make the statement. The eye had been lost to a couple of boys who'd tried to rob him on his way home from the currency exchange one day a year ago. Luckily, they didn't get much money for their trouble, but he paid the price with a knife-stab in the eye. He never wore a patch over it because he didn't want to remind himself that the eye was dead. Neither did he want to remind anybody else that he was blind in one eye—that he was handicapped. He'd be a walking victim advertising himself.

Back in his apartment, he searched for a hammer and nails. When he found them, he tacked the sign to the stick. With the poster fastened, he raised it above his head and said with a vengeance, "Rid Maypole Street of Stray Dogs Now!"

At seven o'clock the following morning when he awoke, Fullman Smith sat on the edge of the bed and felt between his mattress and box spring for the .38. When he found it, he went to his dresser drawer, removed the bullets from under a pile of underwear and loaded it carefully. Then he dressed, putting the gun in the waistband of his pants. He slipped on a jacket to conceal the bulge.

As he dressed, he heard Penny in the kitchen cooking breakfast. She never needed to be awakened in the morning. She got up by herself, dressed herself, and fixed breakfast for the two of them.

At nine years of age, she had the precocity usually typical of late-in-life children raised by older parents. She was the kind of child that old folks describe as "having been here before." And, during the past year, Fullman recognized in her a sense of responsibility she felt for him since he'd lost the eye. He needed her as much as she needed him and he suspected she knew it.

As he sat down before the toast, sausage, eggs, and coffee she had prepared for him, he felt jittery, as though an electric current ran through his arteries. He hoped Penny didn't sense it.

"I'm takin' you to school today, Baby," he said.

Penny didn't reply. She nodded her head in a way that said she knew why he was taking her to school, and that she knew what would happen once he left her and came home; an all-knowing nod, the kind that often frightens adults because they can't fathom the labyrinths of a child's mind.

After eating, he went to the window that overlooked the empty lot and counted seven dogs as they foraged among the litter of leftover scraps of food thrown from car windows.

He left the apartment with the sign in one hand and Penny's hand in the other. Outside, as they crossed the street on the side where the dogs were, he felt her hand tremble.

"It's all right, Baby," he said.

A black dog sauntered up to them, sniffing at his pantleg as if trying to decide whether to allow the two of them the use of the sidewalk. Fullman could see the ragged edge of where half the dog's ear had been chewed off. Drawing back the sign, he swung it at the animal's head and the dog backed off, baring its yellowed fangs.

When they arrived at the school, Fullman released Penny onto the playground and checked his watch. It was seven forty-five.

Taking the same route home, he walked faster in an effort to beat the cameras to the scene. As he turned the corner of his block, he could see that some of the dogs had left and only four were at the site. When he got closer, he recognized the one that had attacked Penny—a German Shepherd mixed with something else. It was nosing through empty fast food bags. Another dog, a brown one that seemed to be kin to a collie, had raised its leg and urinated against the wall of an abandoned building next to the lot. Fullman Smith waited for one of them to approach with its canines bared but not one of them did.

The two other dogs that were on the lot, a male and a female, began to mate. The sight of the dogs mating—two animals that served no purpose that Fullman could explain, triggered an impulse in him that made him pull out the gun and fire two bullets into their necks. They fell over in a heap, still engaged. Next, he turned the gun on the other two who didn't seem to have the good sense to try to run and shot them on the spot. The body of one quivered with life before he emptied the gun and put it back in his waistband.

It was eight o'clock but there was still no one at the scene but himself. Even after ten minutes had passed, still no sign of a television camera. With his bare hands, he dragged the brown and black dogs, dropping each into a heap on top of the other two. With a brick that he found among the rubble on the lot, he drove his sign into the dirt next to them.

Before leaving the scene, he looked at the lifeless carcasses, feeling no more remorse than if he'd squashed a roach. He felt nothing except maybe relief. It was the same feeling he had when Penny's mother and grandmother had left him.

His thoughts moved from his wife and daughter to Bobbie Hale, Joe Pincham, and Lona Mason. All of them were dead to him; as dead as the animals that lay at his feet. The only person who was alive in his thoughts was Penny, and she was alive because there was still hope for her, even though there might not be any left for him. It was only because of that hope that Fullman Smith could live with the person he'd become. He turned away from the dead dogs and went to call the city to remove them before a stench set in.

1979

A Woman's Place

MAE-RUTH RIDLEY TIED ON HER FIGHTING APRON—the red one with the silk-screened devil holding a trident and the words "To hell with housework!" embossed above the hem. Standing over the kitchen stove, she stirred the pot of leftover black-eyed peas, the flabbiness of her upper arm swinging with each turn of the spoon. It was like a relay race, only without a partner for the hand-off—hard for her to believe that she had just finished her fourth week as a catalog order filler for Sears Roebuck's mail order house and was now standing over a hot kitchen range cooking her family's supper.

Counting the overtime, the job paid well for an unskilled worker, and Mae-Ruth was thankful to have gotten hired. After all, her son Ezell needed school clothes and she needed a new winter coat, but most of all she wanted to help her husband Cecil buy a home in a better neighborhood where she could walk the street safely. Cecil couldn't do it alone, even though he moonlighted as a security guard, so Mae-Ruth took it upon herself to get out and find a job.

Too proud to admit that the help was needed, Cecil nearly brought down the roof when she announced that she'd joined the ranks of the employed.

"A woman's place is in the home!" he ranted, stamping his foot as though Mae-Ruth was supposed to retreat like a scared mouse back into the woodwork. "Why you think I'm working two jobs?"

"When your paychecks are big enough for us to get the things we need, I'll gladly sit at home," she replied, knowing full well that it was the biggest lie she'd yet told. Now that she had gotten used to working and having her own spending money, she would never be content to stay at home and be a housewife. One month in the workforce taught her that a wife's place in a household could not be dictated by her husband. She had to choose her own place. Mae-Ruth had chosen hers, and it was up to Cecil to accept it.

Cecil Ridley had no comeback. It was clear that his two jobs still weren't enough to keep the family even with inflation. The fact that his wife nearly earned as much with her steady overtime as he did on his regular job added insult to injury. But in order to impress upon her that his acquiescence hadn't been won without a concession from her, Cecil made Mae-Ruth promise to have a hot meal on the table when he came home between jobs. She had kept up her end of the bargain, albeit with some difficulty.

Her first week on the job, Mae-Ruth let it slip that she had been followed home from work by a man who'd gotten off the Homan Avenue bus at her stop. Of course, she had her wits about her so she didn't enter her own dark hallway but walked as fast as her legs could carry her to a neighbor's and leaned on the doorbell until someone answered. The strategy worked, and the man ran down the street.

Cecil cited the incident as one more reason why Mae-Ruth needed to quit, but when she swore that she'd go to work armed if she had to, he grudgingly bought her a small-caliber pistol with an imitation pearl handle. She kept it on her at all times when she had to come home after dark. Fortunately, she hadn't had to use it. She hoped she'd never have to.

She went to a cabinet and took the plates out, setting them in their proper positions on the table and adding to the setting a knife, fork, and spoon. Next, she went to the kitchen door to call Cecil to the table. He was getting dressed for the second job, putting on a faded blue security guard's uniform.

Mae-Ruth eyed him as he fastened the holster that held the unloaded .22 he wore around his waist. To her way of thinking, carrying an unloaded gun was humiliating. Cecil couldn't even defend himself if push came to shove. But the company that he worked for refused to be liable for any trigger-happy security guards creating lawsuits that they'd have to fork over money for. Mae-Ruth believed they were too cheap to bond the door shakers they hired out. She knew it bothered Cecil, though he never said much about it. It had to make him feel like a paper tiger when his own son asked him why he walked around carrying a gun without any bullets.

She sent him to find Ezell so they could eat. When she heard the door slam, she spooned the peas onto each plate, putting a larger portion on Cecil's. Mae-Ruth couldn't understand how he could eat more than she did but never seemed to gain an ounce, but though she ate like a bird, she'd gain enough for him and her both. Ashamed of her weight, she had discussed it with her mother once and was told that nobody wanted a bone but a dog and that even it likes meat on it most of the time. Mae-Ruth laughed whenever her mother would say it, but she still wasn't satisfied. It was one more reason why she was glad to be working. By working, she burned up more calories. If she sat at home, she'd be watching the stories, feeling sorry for herself, and eating more than she knew she should.

Placing a slice of cornbread on each plate, she poured milk into each of the three glasses. Though she had worked up an appetite, she never touched a crumb until Cecil and Ezell were seated at the table. She couldn't enjoy her meal unless she could watch them fill their mouths with the food she'd cooked.

❖

Half an hour had passed since she'd sent Cecil out to get Ezell and she worried about what was taking them so long. Cecil often told her she was too protective of the boy. If it had been up to her, he argued, Ezell would stay cooped up in the apartment when he came home from school until she came home from work. On the other hand, Mae-Ruth felt that she had to be protective. Cecil was always at work and seemed to never have time for Ezell. In the mornings when Ezell got up, Cecil would have already left the house. He spent a hot minute with the boy when he'd rush home between jobs to eat, and by the time he got off the second job, Ezell was usually sound asleep.

Mae-Ruth spent some time with him, but it wasn't the same as him being with his father. She couldn't discuss the things that occupied the mind of a thirteen-year-old boy, or help him build the model cars that she tripped over when she entered his bedroom. When she got home herself, she was practically dead on her feet—too tired to supervise his activities. Her only way of exercising some control over Ezell was to constantly keep tabs on him. But she could only watch him so far, and lately, he had been showing signs of rebelliousness. She had her suspicions that he was being influenced by the gang members who lived on the block.

She had rued the day that the family moved to the West Side of Chicago and had remained unconvinced that it was the best place to raise Ezell. But Cecil realized that Arkansas couldn't give him the opportunity to provide for his family like he wanted to despite the fact that he wanted Ezell to experience the kind of boyhood he had in the South. He and Mae-Ruth wanted the best of both worlds, but they had to make a choice. Mae-Ruth realized that in choosing the East Garfield Park neighborhood of Chicago, that they had picked the worst of the two.

She soon heard Cecil's knock at the door. He had forgotten his house keys. At times he was as bad as Ezell—she had two children on her hands instead of one. She let him in.

"Where's Ezell?" she asked.

"I don't know, Baby," Cecil replied. "Went over to the schoolyard, but he wasn't there. I went by his friend Jimmy's, but Jimmy ain't seen him. I don't know where he could be. But he can't be too far. I'm gonna whip him like a yard dog when he turns up."

"That's the trouble with him now," Mae-Ruth answered. "The only way you know how to communicate with him is to whip him. There's more to being a father than that..."

"I don't need you telling me how to be a father," Cecil said, pointing a finger in her face. "Especially when you ain't doing such a bang-up job of being a mother yourself."

"I 'magine your idea of a good mother is one that's got her belly poking out nine months outta every year," Mae countered.

Cecil didn't answer. Mae-Ruth watched him go into the kitchen, pull out a chair and sit down to eat by himself.

To her, the family meal was inviolable. It was as sacred as the wafer and wine of communion. A meal wasn't nourishing if a person had to eat alone—out of the company of the family that he was supposed to share love and faith with. Dinnertime was the time to talk about the day's blessings and defeats, its promises and denials. It was the only time during the day that Cecil was able to spend with his son, and he seemed content to eat without him, or her, for that matter.

She watched the door of the apartment, consumed by frightening thoughts. She feared the gang had gotten hold of Ezell. He always talked about the pressure he was under to join and about how he had to pay protection dues out of his lunch money. And yet the police couldn't or wouldn't do anything about it—at least not until someone got hurt. In her mind, Mae-Ruth went over Ezell's life from that day thirteen years ago when he was delivered in a Helena, Arkansas, hospital, to that morning when she had sent him off to school. The jarring ring of the telephone brought her back to the present. It rang another time before she answered it.

"Yes, this is Ezell Ridley's house," she told the voice on the other line. "Is he all right, officer? We'll be down right away." She hung the phone up.

"Ezell's down at the Kedzie Avenue station," she told Cecil. "The police caught him with some boys trying to break into a house." It was all she said.

❖

On the way to the police station, Mae-Ruth couldn't talk and Cecil wouldn't. To her it was as if each blamed the other for the trouble that Ezell had gotten into.

"We've got to support one another on this," Cecil said finally, as the car pulled in front of the station. It won't do Ezell a bit of good if we' not together on this."

Tears flooded Mae-Ruth's eyes and rolled down her cheeks. A policeman led them to the detention room where Ezell was being held. It was Mae-Ruth's first time in a police station, and as she watched the officers in a bustle of activity, she compared their crisp blue shirts, razor-creased trousers, and shoes shining like new money to Cecil's dull, ill-fitting security guard uniform.

Ezell had been crying. He sat in a hard-backed chair in the corner of the room.

"Ezell, you got some explaining to do to me and your mother," Cecil said.

"I didn't do it by myself," he said. "They put me up to crawling into the window and breaking in. They said they'd kill me if I didn't." He was distraught.

"Who is *they?*" Cecil asked.

"Danny Lyles and his gang, the Four Corners," Ezell said.

"Don't he live down near the end of the block?" Mae-Ruth asked.

Ezell nodded his head.

Cecil turned to one of the policemen.

"Is he still here?" Cecil asked.

"He's been released to his mother, pending a hearing," the policeman said.

"I'd like to know what kind of mother she is that lets him run the streets influencing other's kids," Mae-Ruth said.

"Probably one that's…"

Mae-Ruth's fierce glare stopped Cecil in mid-sentence.

Ezell was released after his parents signed papers. They were assured that he wouldn't be given a record since it was his first offense.

On the way home, Cecil set the conditions of Ezell's punishment. His allowance was taken from him, and he was grounded—not to leave the house after he came home from school. Mae-Ruth wanted to know who'd be around to enforce the law. Cecil pulled the car up to the apartment building where they lived.

"We've got some talking to do when I get off tonight Mae-Ruth," he said.

"Do you mean to tell me you intend to report for work after your child's just had a brush with the law? You not staying home at least one evening so we can straighten this thing out?"

"Our bills can't go unpaid just 'cause Ezell's had a run-in with the law. I can't tell the people at the plant that I had to stay home 'cause my boy got in trouble. They're depending on me…"

"Well, we depend on you too," Mae-Ruth raised her voice, waving toward the backseat to include Ezell, who, still whimpering, hugged his knees to his chest. "But maybe that's the whole problem. We depend on you too much. Maybe it's time we depended on ourselves." She yanked on the door handle to let herself out.

"What's that supposed to mean?" Cecil asked.

"You figure it out," Mae-Ruth said. "You seem to have all the answers. Come on, Ezell," she said, slamming the car door hard.

Upstairs in the apartment, she got to the window just in time to see Cecil pull off. She turned from the parted curtains and, removing her coat, went to the kitchen to reheat Ezell's dinner.

She couldn't eat. How could she after what she had just gone through? Shaking a Tums from a bottle, she popped it into her mouth and chewed it hungrily in an effort to sedate her churning insides.

"You' big enough to dish up your own food," she told Ezell angrily. "I've gotta make a run. I'll be back in a few minutes. You'd better not leave this house. Do you hear me?" she said.

"Yes, Momma," Ezell said.

Struggling into her coat, Mae-Ruth hurried out of the apartment. In the hallway, she unzipped the small change purse that contained the gun. Holding the weapon in the palm of her hand, she examined it under the dim hall light. Her hand shook as she studied the small pistol. With its imitation pearl handle, it resembled an oversized piece of jewelry—a brooch patterned after a pistol rather than a real weapon. She knew exactly where Danny Lyles lived. Since Cecil wouldn't, she'd see to it herself that he stayed at his end of the block and left her son alone.

As she entered the dark street—a street that was as much a stranger to her as the city seemed to be itself, Mae-Ruth feared nothing, a feeling that was entirely new to her.

When she reached the end of the block, she entered the hallway of Danny's building. No names were on the bells, and the electrical wiring was exposed anyway. If it took her knocking on every door, she would do it.

She rapped on the first one and waited for a response, her hand steady on the gun in her pocket. A young woman opened the door and peeped out.

"I want to know where Danny Lyles lives," Mae-Ruth said.

"On the third floor," the woman said before slamming the door in Mae-Ruth's face.

She climbed the stairs to the third floor and knocked on the door, waiting for an answer, hoping that Danny himself would be bold enough to answer. Inside her coat pocket, her index finger gripped the trigger ring. For her own precaution, the safety was still on, but she wouldn't be afraid to release it, wouldn't balk at holding the muzzle against Danny's head to make him stay away from Ezell.

"Who's knocking?" a woman's reedy voice inquired.

"I want to talk to Danny Lyles," Mae-Ruth replied. "This is Mae-Ruth Ridley from down the street."

A woman about her age stared at her when the door eased open.

"Come in," she said.

"I'm Ezell Ridley's mother," Mae-Ruth continued. "My son's the boy Danny Lyle's been after to join his gang."

"I've seen you a few times on the street," the woman acknowledged.

"I came here to tell your son to stay away from Ezell. Me and my husband had to go down to the Kedzie Avenue station to get him outta trouble—trouble your son caused."

"I don't have no son. All I got is girls," the woman said.

"Ain't Danny Lyles your son?" Mae-Ruth asked. "Why'd you answer the door if he isn't?"

"He stays here sometimes, but I'm tired of claiming him as a child of mine. I gave up on him a long time ago. I've changed the locks on my door so he can't get in. I've put him out any number of times, but when he wants to get in, he breaks in like he does any other place that's got something he wants."

Mae-Ruth grew weak in the knees and sat down on the couch next to her.

"The police said they released him to you. You telling me he ain't here?"

"They didn't release him to me. Somebody else must've got him out, 'tending they was me. I can't do nothing with him. I ask myself if it wouldn't have been better for me to draw welfare instead of getting out working

61

everyday—least maybe I could've kept better track of him. But it's too late for me to know now. I've got three others to think about. Three girls—*good* girls. I guess three outta four ain't so bad..."

"I came here to make Danny Lyles leave Ezell alone," Mae-Ruth said. "I came here with a gun my husband bought me to carry to and from work," she said, pulling it from her coat pocket and showing it to the woman, who showed no expression when she looked at it.

"I lie in my bed many a night, worrying and wondering when the morgue'll call me down to 'dentify him. I know it's bound to happen, and he ain't but fifteen years old." She held her weathered hands up to her face, the long thin fingers pressed against her eyes as if to force out the vision of what her fears wrought.

"I'm sorry," Mae-Ruth apologized. "So help me, I'm sorry."

She put the gun back in her pocket and stood up, but her legs grew wobbly under her. She wanted to comfort the woman, a mother just like she was, wanted to draw her close so that she could absorb some of the pain she was feeling. She wished that she could reassure her that everything would turn out all right, that her son Danny would change. But she couldn't. She was powerless in the matter.

"I've gotta go," she said, her voice faltering. "Please forgive me," she said.

She hurried down the stairs and out into the street, running for the first time she could remember in a long time. When she reached the front of her building, she stopped abruptly, walked to the curb and, reaching into her pocket, pulled out the gun. Holding it above the sewer grating, Mae-Ruth slipped it through one of the slots and heard it splash into the water below.

Ezell was asleep when she returned to the apartment, and it was well past midnight when Cecil put his key into the lock. Mae-Ruth ran to the door before he could get inside.

"We've gotta talk, Cecil," she said. "It can't wait. We've gotta talk right now."

"All right, Mae-Ruth," he said. "Give me a chance to get out of my uniform."

In their bedroom, Cecil lay each article of clothing across the bed as Mae-Ruth talked. It was a ritual that he performed every night when he got off work.

"I went down to Danny Lyles', this evening and talked to his mother," she began. "Oh Cecil, I can't end up like her, regretting things I didn't do for Ezell, things I'm supposed to do as a mother. I'm not go'n live with that kind of guilt on my head..."

"It wasn't your place to go down there," Cecil said. "I'm the one who should've gone."

He placed the shirt and tie on a wire hanger. The shirt was puckered where the badge had once been. He lay his creaseless trousers across the foot of the bed.

"I won't end up with a child who's go'n cause me grief," Mae-Ruth continued.

"You can't control that," Cecil said. "I know lots of families where the kids caused the parents grief, and the parents had nothing to do with it."

"Stop contradicting me and listen, Cecil," she pleaded. "I'm not go'n have a child cause me heartache. If he do, it won't be because I didn't do everything I could to prevent it. I'm quitting my job tomorrow," she announced, folding her arms across her chest. "I've made up my mind."

Cecil, in his underwear, hands on his waist, stared at her.

"What brought this on?" he asked. "You wasn't quitting for nothing and nobody, remember?"

"I never said I wanted to quit, but I've got priorities, and Ezell's the main one."

"All of a sudden, you've got priorities," Cecil said.

For the first time, Mae-Ruth examined the paraphernalia Cecil had spread out on the bed. The gun and holster were missing. Cecil usually lay them on the bed with his cap, belt, and tie.

"Where's your gun and holster?" she asked. "Did they take your *gun* away from you?"

"I turned it in," Cecil told her. "Got tired of carryin' an unloaded gun, so I went to the office and turned it in. I'd have turned in the uniform if I'd had a change of clothes with me. I'm turning it in tomorrow."

"I don't want you quittin' on account of me," Mae-Ruth said. "I was wrong about the things I said today, and I'm sorry."

"I'm quittin' for the family's sake, Mae-Ruth," Cecil replied.

"But you don't have to," Mae-Ruth explained. "That's what I've been trying to tell you all along. I'm the one who's quitting."

The quarrel was turning into a good-natured one that the two of them often had when each would end up assuming the blame for the other.

"It's a done deal," Cecil said, sitting on the edge of the bed in his tee shirt, briefs, and socks. He slowly pulled one sock off, then the other. "You can keep your job as part of the bargain."

"You know that gun you bought me?" Mae-Ruth asked.

"Yeah. You fool around and lose it?" Cecil asked.

Mae-Ruth thought a second before recounting the experience she had at Danny Lyles's. She thought he should know, knew that he had a right to know, but couldn't bring herself to tell him.

"Yeah, I lost it. I must've lost it somewhere in the street," she said.

"Well, it wasn't registered anyway," Cecil said. "I guess that makes us even. I can pick you up from work from now on instead of you taking the bus."

"That'll be good," Mae-Ruth replied. "I never liked riding the bus anyway."

1981

Trapped

IN MARCH, when she got the Chicago postmarked letter, Evvie Love thought her sister Corene had sent it. After all, she didn't know a soul in Chicago—at least no one who would have had cause to write her. And Corene rarely wrote, either because of laziness, or preoccupation, or both, yet Evvie couldn't cast any stones because she wasn't a faithful letter writer herself. Despite the infrequent letters that found their way to her mailbox, Evvie knew Corene's handwriting when she saw it, and the envelope was written in an unfamiliar hand. It took her all of a minute to figure out that her nephew Dade, Corene's thirty-year-old son had written it. Fingering open the flap, Evvie read the news that Corene, whom she hadn't seen in ten years, had a nervous breakdown.

The news stunned her as Evvie stood in her living room rereading the words as if there were some hidden message she still hadn't decoded. Corene, the more headstrong of the two girls who had left Mississippi thirty years before for a better life in Chicago was cracking up. It took her son Dade to write the letter asking that Evvie come North: the poor thing probably couldn't put a pen to paper herself. Shutting her eyes to stave off the tears, Evvie rebuked herself for tarrying when she should have been making preparations to leave Greenville that minute.

As if under the grip of mind control, Evvie went to her closet, dragged a trunk from its corner and began snatching clothes from hangers. After a brief inspection of each garment, she tossed it into the open trunk.

The trip required that she draw money out of her bank account, and she would have to add to it the money she took in from ironing for white families in town. The train usually left the station at noon or close to it, and she could expect to arrive in Chicago before dawn the next morning. She would have to ask Cleve Barton, her nearest neighbor, to take her into town. Last minute details ran through Evvie's head as she dragged out and packed every imagined necessity that would make her trip to Chicago comfortable.

"Don't worry 'bout a thing," Rose Barton said when Evvie told them that she was going to Chicago to visit her sick sister. "Cleve 'n me'll take care of everything. Have a safe trip. We'll pray for you, Ev," she promised.

Evvie thanked her. The Bartons were as much kin to her as if their blood ran through her veins.

Cleve followed Evvie into her house. His two hundred-odd pounds stuffed in denim coveralls, he lowered his bulk onto the trunk's lid while Evvie flipped the heavy brass locks and secured them with the key.

As he lugged the trunk through the house and hoisted it over the tailgate of his station wagon, Evvie took her gilt-edged Bible from the dresser and clutched it to her bosom.

"Send me up North as a Christian, Lord. Give me the strength to face the trials I'm go'n meet up there. Help me to get there in one piece so I can be in a shape to help Corene. Amen."

Running a comb through her tightly-curled hair, she dusted her face with powder and tugged at the inseams of her dress, pulling it closer to her knees. Grabbing an atomizer from the top of her dresser, she squirted a jet of rose-scented toilet water behind each ear. Her makeover was complete after she traced her lips red and penciled two eyebrows onto a bald forehead.

Before her exit, she paused to look around the four-room cottage as if to bid the walls farewell, then locked the door.

"Be seein' you soon, Ev," Rose said, hugging her. "Give my love to Corene... if she remembers me," she added.

"She'll remember you, Rose," Evvie said. "Nobody can forget a person as kind as you. Don't forget to tend to my plants, Rose. I don't want 'em dying on me while I'm gone."

Going to Cleve's car, she took a deep breath before getting in. Spring looked as if it were coming early that March. It had rained that morning and the humid air was laden with the scent of pines and evergreen shrubs that surrounded the house. The heavy sweetness of the air seemed to coat Evvie's palate as she breathed it in. She climbed into the Ford, her eyes fixed on the grayish-white house that she'd occupied for the last thirty years. The rear tires of the Ford spit up a cloud of dust as Cleve Barton sped off to catch the train to Chicago.

The train ride to Chicago was a tortuous one with frequent stops to southern hamlets to pick up emigrants leaving the South. As the stark scenery reeled past her eyes, Evvie began to worry about her sister. Her heart seemed to throb in time with the rhythmic clatter of the train wheels over the tracks.

Why was Corene suffering? Evvie wondered. Was she working herself too hard? She had a habit of letting her work get the best of her and the possibility of her overworking herself wasn't out of the question. No, it had to be the environment, Evvie concluded. Had to be. She'd visited Corene a few times in Chicago and each visit nearly threw her into a state of depression: the filth of the neighborhoods, the coldness of the people, the hostility. So, instead of visiting her sister, she resorted to calling every now and then until Corene's phone got cut off. And then Evvie couldn't understand why two working people couldn't keep a phone on but she never broached the subject in the few letters she wrote. She didn't want to hurt her sister's feelings.

❖

The train arrived in Chicago at three A.M. Evvie had catnapped on and off during the ride—worry had robbed her of a decent night's rest and she was wide awake, staring out the window, probing the black void that was night for answers to her questions.

As soon as she got off, the cold Chicago air hit her in the face. Standing behind a pillar that blocked the wind, she waited for her luggage to be unloaded. Drawing her coat closer to her, she watched as reunited kin embraced and kissed each other. In each jubilant woman she saw Corene's face and Evvie laughed and cried inwardly anticipating the joy of their reunion.

She had no one to meet her at the station, which was just as well since she didn't want to be the cause of dragging anyone out of bed. Besides, she hadn't given Dade a chance to expect a reply.

She flagged a Checker cab that was parked outside, its motor running, the exhaust a white streak in the March cold. The driver got out, lugged her trunk into the taxi and climbed in behind the wheel.

"Where can I take you, Ma'am?" he asked, slamming the meter flag down.

"I'm going to 1730 Walnut Street. You know where that is don't you?" she asked.

"I don't usually go into that part of the city this time of night—it's kinda dangerous," he explained, "but seein' as you come a long distance, I'll make an exception."

"I 'preciate it," Evvie replied, "but I'd thank you to name me one place up here that *ain't* dangerous."

"Where you from?" he asked, declining to meet her challenge.

"I'm from the Old Country," she said laughing. "Cain't you tell?"

"What part of the Old Country?" the man asked, speeding along the streets of the factory district just west of downtown.

"Greenville, Mississippi," she answered. She then rifled through her pocketbook, searching for her coin purse. She had been watching the periodic clicks of the meter since she entered the cab and wanted to have her fare in hand when she reached her destination.

"Well I'll be," the cabbie shot out. "I'm from near there myself."

"Wherebouts?" Evvie asked, leaning forward in her seat.

"Ever heard of a place called Belzoni?" he asked.

"Who you asking?" she retorted. "I been to Belzoni many times—ain't too many places in Mississippi I ain't been..."

"Sometimes I wish I was back there now," the cabbie said.

"I bet you do. It's just so much happening up here 'til it ain't no wonder my sister's taken sick."

"Sorry to hear that, Ma'am," the driver said.

"Evvie Love—the name's Evvie Love," she introduced herself. "That's the reason I'm up here—my nephew wrote and sent for me. She been down in her back for a week now..."

"That's too bad," the cabbie said. "To tell the truth, Chicago ain't done me such a bad turn. I makes a pretty good buck—better 'n what I would make if I'd stayed in Mississippi."

"You just said you 'fraid to go into your own neighborhoods at night—it ain't that way where I'm from..."

"Well you know how black folks are sometimes... Some of 'em ain't got nothin', don't want nothin', and wants to knock you in the head to take what little you got."

"I imagine they's in such a rut until the only thing they can do is strike out at they own. White folks ain't go'n let 'em get close enough to them—that's for sho," Evvie Love said, shaking her head.

The streets were barren at that hour in the morning, and hot white steam rose from the sewers and faded in the cold night air.

With a blast from the engine, the taxi pulled in front of the run-down apartment building. On one landing a hall light was burning. A stray cat perched in the basement window of the building, shivering and caterwauling in the cold. The window was coated with a thin, silvery sheet of ice and the diffused light of a lamp glowed through, highlighting frosted designs on the pane.

Evvie Love fingered the loose coins in her change purse.

"What do I owe you? Eight fifty-five?" she answered her own question. She separated a ten dollar bill from the other bills in her purse. "Keep the change," she said.

The cabbie let her out and went to the trunk to remove her baggage. Grasping the trunk by the handle, he dragged it to the stoop and sat it down. Evvie stood at the door.

"Wait a minute," she said grinning. "Ain't you 'fraid to go into there?"

The cabbie looked at Evvie and shook his head in a laugh.

"If you ain't scared, I certainly ain't, Miz Love," he said.

She pushed the door open and he struggled up the stairs with the trunk.

"We only goin' to the first floor," she told him.

At the head of the stairs, the cabbie sat the trunk down, Evvie close on his heels.

"Thank you, Sir," she said. "Never did get your name."

"Just call me 'Old Country'," he replied with a laugh.

"Old Country," she addressed him. "Tell me why you went to all this trouble for a worrisome old lady like me."

"You a home girl, Miz Love," he replied. "No matter how hard this cab business has made me, I cain't forsake anybody from the Old Country."

She chuckled at being called a girl.

"I'm glad to know there's some people up here who care 'bout somebody 'sides just theyselves."

The cabbie ran down the stairs, his footsteps a deafening flurry in the quiet hall. Evvie heard him slam the cab door and speed off.

Evvie knocked on the door to her sister's apartment. There was no answer. Knocking a second time, harder than the first, she reassured herself that she was at the right apartment. Corene was in no position to have moved since her last visit. Maybe she should have notified them so that they would've been expecting her. But she liked to spring surprises. Yet Evvie couldn't go anywhere if no one answered the door. She had no place to go—knew no one else in Chicago, so she'd have to wait. Dade would answer the door, she thought. He had to be there. He wouldn't leave his mother alone in her condition, Evvie reasoned.

Rattling the doorknob, she waited for a reply, her heart heaving inside her breast. Soon, she heard a stirring inside as a loosened floor board creaked over a joist.

"Who is it?" a man's mildly cross voice asked.

"It's Evvie. Your Aunt Evvie Love!" she answered strongly.

He cracked the door, peeped out, and flung it open wide when he recognized her. He stared at her in disbelief. His eyes were glassy and set deep in his face.

Evvie threw herself at him, hugging his long, frail body. His brownish hair was wild and wiry and his yellow skin looked unhealthy.

"Aunt Evvie," he said as if he couldn't believe who she was.

Evvie's teary eyes clouded the lens of her glasses in the cold hall.

"Look at you, Dade," she said. "Boy, you don growed. Give your old auntie a hug. My, ain't you raily, though. Been eatin' too much of that poor Northern food—that's why... but Aunt Evvie'll fatten you up directly... Where's Corene? Where's my sister?" she asked.

"She's in her room... in bed, Aunt Evvie. Flat on her back like she been for two weeks... Let me help you with that trunk," he offered, as if in an afterthought.

He tugged at it, and, after considerable strain, got it into the apartment.

Evvie glanced around the room as Dade moved the trunk to a corner. Nothing had changed. The same dark green drapes hung from a rod above the window. The old, cracked walls wore the same dull coat of green-gray paint.

She went to the bedroom door, put her ear to it, and nudged it. It squeaked as she nudged it ajar. She walked in, looking in the dark toward the bed. Corene lay under a blanket, her thin body forming a long low mound. Evvie couldn't see her face. On tiptoe, she stole over to the bed, the floor boards creaking under her feet. Corene stirred on the bed, above the squeaking bedsprings.

"Dade," Corene called out in a low moan.

"Corene, Honey, it ain't nobody but me," Evvie whispered as her fingers grazed her sister's hand.

Terrified, Corene recoiled and bounded to a sitting position on the bed. Her eyes snapped open and she shivered, shaking the mattress.

"Corene! Corene!" Evvie cried. "It's me, Evvie!"

"Evvie who?" Corene asked. "I don't know no Evvie."

"It's me, Corene. Your sister. I came up here to see 'bout you—Dade sent for me."

"I tell you I don't know no Evvie. Pull the chain light to the ceiling—let me see you with my own eyes."

Evvie pulled the chain and the bulb threw a dim yellow light making the two sisters visible to each other for the first time in ten years.

"Evvie, is that you?" Corene asked. She pulled Evvie down on the bed, her long arms hugging Evvie's neck. Tears rolled down Evvie's cheeks and met under her chin.

"My sister—my onliest sister!" Evvie cried.

Suddenly, Corene let go and turned her back to Evvie.

"You came here to pity me—your hankty, long lost sister... Well, look at me!" Corene shrieked. "Look at what a nervous wreck I am!"

"Corene, I come here to help you get well. You my sister," Evvie consoled her.

"I ain't myself, Evvie... I'm confused...I didn't mean it. Don't leave me," she cried. Her bony knees tented the blanket in a weak attempt to sit up.

"Lie on back, Corene," Evvie said. "I'll be here for a while. Don't fret," she calmed her sister, looking into the coon-like circles around Corene's eyes. "I'm going to unpack now," she said. "I'll be right in the next room if you need me." Evvie turned off the light and walked out, shaking her head. Tears fell onto the carpet.

She would take Corene home. Back to the Old Country. That was all there was to it. Corene couldn't recuperate and regain her senses in the environment she was in—in a dark room with a man to look after her. Evvie had brought enough money for two fares back to Mississippi, where the air was fresh and the people were her kin.

Dade sat in a chair in the living room, nodding and blinking his eyes as though catching up on a week's loss of sleep.

"Dade, go back to bed an' get you some rest," Evvie ordered, sniffling. "I'm here now."

When she awoke the next morning and went to Corene's room to tell her of the plan to take her home, Dade was gone. Evvie shook Corene to rouse her and Corene sprang forward as if prodded by a shock.

"Corene, I made up my mind," Evvie said. "I'm taking you home tomorrow. The sooner I get you 'way from here, the sooner you can get back on your feet. I brought enough money for your ticket. I won't take no for an answer."

"Where's Dade?" Corene asked, training her dull eyes on Evvie.

"He got out early this morning—'fore day, I guess," Evvie replied. "Where's he working, Corene?"

"He ain't working no place but in the streets," Corene answered. "Get your purse," she ordered.

"Why?" Evvie asked. "You need money?"

"Get your pocketbook!" Corene demanded.

Evvie went to her room and brought out her old black vinyl handbag.

"You need money?" she asked. "Tell me how much you need."

She rifled through the handbag looking for her coin purse. Finding it, she pinched open the clasp. The contents were empty. In shock, Evvie held the coin purse up to the light and then rummaged through her pocketbook frantically.

"It ain't there," Corene said.

"What you mean?" Evvie asked.

"I'm telling you it ain't there—Dade took it. He set a trap for you, you took the bait, and fell for it. He knew you'd come up here the minute you found out I was sick... "

"He sent for me to beat me outta my money?" Evvie asked, hit by a truth that her faith couldn't allow her to accept.

"He's done it to me so many times that I couldn't keep count. At times, I'd swear it wasn't him... that I mislaid the money. Didn't want to believe that my own child would steal from me, but he ain't been responsible since he got hooked."

"That's the real reason for your sickness, ain't it Corene?" Evvie asked. "He's worried your nerves raw."

Corene gathered her strength and rose to get out of the bed.

"I ain't go'n take it no more, Evvie," she said. "You go'n help me put a stop to it. I couldn't bring myself to do it, but you go'n do something I ain't had the courage to do."

"I'm go'n put a stop to it all right!" Evvie exclaimed. "We' getting 'way from here. Today. You goin' home with me to 'cuperate. I'm go'n have Cleve wire me some money—I'll pay him back when we get home."

"You ain't listening, Evvie," Corene said. "I said you can stop Dade from stealing. All you got to do is press charges—file a complaint."

"Press charges?" Evvie asked. "'Gainst my own kin?"

"You got to, Evvie," Corene said. "Your kin's forsaken you. You got to press charges."

"But I can't turn him in like he's a stranger—like I don't even know him. Besides, I ain't got proof he took it—it coulda been somebody else. I coulda misplaced it."

"Evvie, if you don't do it, it's just like you encouraging him on. I won't set one foot outside this door if you don't. You can just pack your trunk and leave. I ain't going nowhere until I know he's safe where I don't have to worry 'bout him no more."

"Safe in jail? I can't believe it," Evvie said tearfully. "My own kin. I can't accept it." Tears fell onto Corene's blanket.

"Safe so he can't steal from nobody else."

"Is that grocery store still down there on the corner?" Evvie asked. "If I gotta make a choice, I'm go'n choose whoever'll benefit the most," she said resignedly.

"It's still there," Corene replied. "Help me get dressed. I'm going with you to make that call. I want to hear you file the complaint," she said, rising from the bed. "And it ain't no need of you feeling like no traitor. I'm the traitor. If I hadn't turned my back on my home a long time ago, I wouldn't feel like a stranger going back."

1982

Day Work

NAOMI BROWN DIDN'T READ the *Daily Word* or join in the idle chit-chat of the other domestics who did day work and commuted from Chicago's West Side to the North Shore suburbs; she sat at the back of the el car, tuned out the blaring radios, and studied the music to a piano concerto that she kept at the bottom of her Jewel Foods shopping bag. Had Esther Wolff, her employer, any idea that Naomi stole two hours of each work day to cultivate a musical talent, she'd fire her, or, at worst, would suffer a coronary and join her late husband Myron in Shalom Memorial Park.

In some ways though, she wasn't as bad as the other wealthy people Naomi had worked for: she didn't plant money under couch cushions to test Naomi's honesty, she never used a white glove to evaluate her thoroughness in cleaning, and not once had she set the clocks back to get more than eight hours' work out of Naomi. Yet she did have her peculiarities.

The grand piano that occupied the music room for thirty years had remained silent since Myron Wolff's sudden death three years before. The room, unchanged since the day he died, was treated as a shrine and Naomi's entrance into it other than to put fresh roses there would warrant her dismissal.

But she did enter it. For two hours each day and only Napoleon, Esther Wolff's poodle, knew. But of course, he couldn't talk.

Esther Wolff headed a fund-raising committee whose task it was to raise money for the Myron Wolff Music Wing at Northwestern University. In her opinion, the most appropriate way for him to be remembered on the campus of his alma mater was not by a collection of his famous recordings but by a monument that would remind serious music students of his contribution to classical music. She was given office space to plan a benefit concert that was six months away, a job which required that she contact important names in the classical music world to perform—friends of her late husband.

Naomi, who had been in her employ for two years, sensed an opportunity to bring to light a musical talent that had taken twenty-five years for her to develop. She had kept the ability bottled up like a magnum of vintage champagne, waiting for the right occasion to un-pop the cork to share it with a discerning authority. And Esther Wolff was that authority. She had herself sacrificed a promising concert career so that her husband could become one of the country's virtuoso classical musicians, and because Esther Wolff had been so involved in the tribute to him, Naomi knew that another time would never come for her. Today was the day that she would finally ask Esther Wolff for a hearing to appraise this ability. But she had to handle the situation carefully—as delicately as she handled Esther Wolff's prized crystal objets d'art.

At eight-thirty sharp, Esther Wolff screeched to a halt in the orange Volkswagen that met Naomi at the train each morning. It was a trial for Naomi to squeeze through the narrow opening between the front and back seat to reach the rear of the car while Napoleon sat on the front seat beside Esther Wolff. The two made an odd pair, Naomi thought—Esther Wolff wearing her white cropped hair in a style that resembled the poodle's coat.

During the short ride, she never talked to Naomi, other than to point out a specific chore that needing doing. But this never bothered Naomi. In fact, she preferred it that way. She was content to ride in silence, concentrating on the music to the concerto that she had been practicing for the past few weeks, and, in her mind, she was not being bumped around in the back seat of the car like excess baggage: she was seated in front of a Steinway piano before a capacity-filled audience at Carnegie Hall.

Esther Wolff finally broke the silence.

"Naomi, I'll be home late this afternoon. I left your pay under the vase on the mantel if you have to leave early. I do hope you can stay—you know how I hate for Napoleon to be left alone."

"I can stay longer," Naomi offered, hoping that Esther Wolff would be so late that she could get in an extra hour's playing time at the piano.

"And don't forget to have Abe deliver fresh roses for the music room. The others are wilted," she reminded Naomi.

"I called him yesterday," Naomi said. "He'll be out first thing this morning."

"You keep a step ahead of me, Naomi," Esther Wolff said. "But that's why I hired you. I could tell that you didn't need to be told what to do."

Naomi smiled at the statement.

❖

The Wolff mansion was an ivy-covered colonial—too much house for a widow and a dog. When they reached the gates of the drive, Esther Wolff kissed the dog and handed him to Naomi. Naomi and Napoleon got out and she watched the car creep down the tree-shaded street like a giant ladybug. It was ridiculous for a wealthy widow to drive an old Volkswagen she thought, but the more Naomi considered it, it was really no odder than polishing a male dog's claws red or placing roses on the piano of a man who had been dead for three years.

Upon entering the house, she immediately took her white uniform and shoes from the shopping bag to get the dog-eared music to Chopin's Concerto in E Minor. Slowly, she opened the large doors of the music room. The piano rested on a red-carpeted dais a few feet from the large windows that overlooked the north grounds of the estate.

Lifting the cover, Naomi stared at the ivory keys. Closing her eyes, she limbered her fingers before beginning the concerto, and, after a quick run up the scales, she began to caress them. The melody filled the room, the notes seeming to float on air in rapid succession like a train of delicate soap bubbles. The concerto was a challenge for her to master. Moved by the emotion that the music inspired in her, she stopped and lowered the lid. Her household chores awaited her.

Upstairs, in a bathroom, she slipped on her white uniform and combed out her graying natural. Never had she thought she'd go days without running a hot comb through it but she adopted the style not only because it was simple to take care of but because it was assertive. Esther Wolff didn't like it, of course, and told Naomi that she preferred her hair in the style she used to wear but Naomi didn't change it. Twenty-eight years' experience as a domestic outweighed the need for her to comply with her employer's personal tastes.

Naomi had been told often that she was an attractive woman but only lately had she begun to believe it. Her caramel-smooth complexion was unblemished so she rarely wore makeup. Esther Wolff asked her once why, at Naomi's age, didn't she wrinkle to which she replied that "it must be the Lord's allowance for my being black." She could tell from Esther Wolff's expression that she neither liked the answer nor its obvious truth.

In keeping with her system, Naomi worked the upstairs first. She began by cleaning the bathrooms, which were usually the dirtiest rooms in the house. Then she made up Esther Wolff's bed. Naomi never understood how one person could be so untidy but she soon realized that, with Esther Wolff's money and with someone diligent like herself to clean up behind her, she could afford to be. At times, Naomi had the feeling that Esther Wolff was flaunting her privilege by stepping out of her underwear and leaving it right on the floor where it fell.

After she finished upstairs, Naomi would dust and wax the furniture downstairs, vacuum the carpet, polish the mirrors, and scrub and wax the parquet floors in the foyer, hall, and kitchen if they needed it. After lunch, when the bulk of her chores were completed and the laundry was in the washing machine, she would practice. The only tasks remaining were ironing the clothes, taking Napoleon for his daily walk, and preparing Esther Wolff's dinner, which required a special trip to the grocer since her food had to be kosher.

Napoleon seemed to know when the time for practice arrived as well as she. He would run into the music room, circle the piano, and sit up on hind legs begging for Naomi to play. And no matter how tired she was from the housework, she was refreshed when she sat down at the bench. The stolen sessions were therapy for her, for she had kept alive the belief that, had circumstances been different for her, she might have made a contribution in life; she might have been more than a woman who earned her living by cleaning up after someone else. Besides this though, the very fact that, for two hours out of the day she defied Esther Wolff made the practice session as thrilling as a tightrope walker's performance on a high wire.

Naomi had been at the piano for ninety minutes when she heard the doorbell chime during a break in the music. Jumping up from the bench, she eased the lid down and threw the music into the shopping bag that she kept handy, just in case it was Esther Wolff springing a surprise visit. Through the peephole of the heavy oak door, Naomi saw that it was Abe, the florist. He carried a box of long-stemmed roses She let him in and went to get the money.

"I thought you were coming by earlier," she said. "You're never this late."

"Got tied up," he replied. "You practicing for a recital?" he asked as Naomi gave him the money.

"No!" Naomi blurted. "What makes you ask?" She tried to cover up her surprise.

"I ain't heard music like that coming from this house since old man Wolff died."

"Oh," Naomi said, clapping her hand to her mouth. "That was just a recording I clean house by. They make records so perfect that they sound live—even Ella Fitzgerald can't tell the difference," she lied.

"*She* might not be able to tell but *I* can," Abe said. "Heard concert music like that for too long 'round here."

"But you're mistaken, Abe," Naomi insisted.

"I don't think I am," he contended.

"Esther Wolff put you up to it, didn't she?" she asked finally. "That's why you were so late coming. She sent you here to check up on me."

"Check up on you?" Abe asked.

"I should've known she was up to something," Naomi said. "Telling me she was going to be late coming home. She was setting me up. She sent you here to spy on me."

"You the one who called me to come out," Abe said. "Or have you forgot already? You been working for her too long. It's beginning to rub off." He shook his head.

Naomi could see that he was telling the truth. Of course she had called him the day before, and he said he was coming first thing in the morning like he usually did. But it wouldn't have been unlike Esther Wolff to have called and delayed him so he could hear her practicing. In spite of this, she gave him the benefit of the doubt.

"I'm sorry, Abe," she apologized. "I must've been working too hard. Please don't breathe a word of this to Mrs. Wolff... I might lose my job."

She excused herself and went to the mantel, took a five dollar bill out of her week's pay and forced it into Abe's hand.

"You don't have to worry 'bout a thing," Abe said. "But you ain't s'posed to keep your light under a bushel basket...if you know what I mean."

Naomi smiled and closed the door. She fully realized how stupid she had been for jumping to conclusions. Upset by her encounter with Abe, she was in no frame of mind to return to the piano for the day.

It really hadn't dawned on her that she might be heard. She had taken all necessary precautions. She had closed the doors to the music room and made sure that all the windows were locked. The room was supposed to be soundproofed, or so she thought. If Abe had heard her, then Esther Wolff might have and might just be waiting for the opportunity to catch her in the act. Yet Naomi wanted a hearing on her own terms. She didn't want to be caught red-handed like a thief. She had to prepare Esther Wolff, had to lay the groundwork.

She went to every window in the house to make sure that it was closed. Afterwards, she unwrapped the roses, and, cutting each one at an angle, placed it in a white porcelain vase atop the piano. Having lost her resolve, Naomi decided to postpone her plan to play for Esther Wolff until she was in a better frame of mind. Instead, she would go to the grocery store to get food for Esther Wolff's dinner, hoping that the crisp fall air would help clear her mind. She took off her uniform and folded it, placing it with the shoes and some other items into her shopping bag. She put the bag in a corner of the foyer so she wouldn't forget it when she left for the evening. When Napoleon ran to the door, expecting to go out, she chased him away and closed the door.

Half an hour later, when she returned with a small bag of groceries, Esther Wolff met Naomi at the door. Naomi was startled to find her home so early.

"I expected you home later," she told her. "I haven't even cooked your dinner yet."

She went to a table to put the groceries down and immediately noticed her shoes, uniform, and the rest of the bag's contents lying on the floor. Esther Wolff brought the sheet music from behind her back, shaking the sheets in Naomi's face.

"What's the meaning of this?" she demanded.

"Abe told you, didn't he?" Naomi asked.

"Abe told me nothing," Esther Wolff replied. "Napoleon, who's not to be left alone in the first place, was nosing around in that bag and got ahold of your shoes. When I went to put them back, I found this music. I demand an explanation."

"It's a piece I've been practicing," Naomi answered calmly.

"Not on Myron's piano!" Esther Wolff shouted. "When I hired you, I forbade you to enter that room... Why you deceitful!" She lunged at Naomi.

Naomi backed away.

"Yes! I played the piano," she retorted. "Every day since I've been here."

Esther Wolff turned as white as Naomi's shoes.

"Get out before I have you arrested!"

She went to the phone.

"Get out!" she screamed.

"I'll leave, but not before I say what I have to," Naomi replied.

Esther Wolff, too shaken to dial the number, slammed the receiver down.

"You have nothing to tell me," she said. "Nothing!" she repeated, putting her hands over her ears.

"I played that piano behind your back because I had to," Naomi began. "I had to prove something to myself. I cheated myself out of a career in music. When my mother scrubbed floors to save the money to start me in music school, I ran off and got married. My husband argued that a career in classical music was hopeless, a pipe dream, and I believed him. When he left me with three kids to support and no job skills, I had to make it the best way I could—by doing day work. But one morning when the kids were still young, I decided that I was going back to my music come hell or high water." She laughed bitterly.

"I took lessons and made sure that every person I kept house for owned a piano. For twenty-five years I made sure that my employers met my requirements like I had to meet theirs."

"But you had no right," Esther Wolff cut in. "You... had... no... right... ." Each word was spoken with equal emphasis.

"I followed your husband's career. No one ever suspected that I appreciated classical music. When he played at the Opera House, I saved up a week's pay to buy a ticket, but was told that they were all sold out, and when I had heard by word-of-mouth that you were looking for a housekeeper, it was the chance I had waited years for. Do you think I applied for work here because I needed a job? I quit the job I had so I could work for you. I prayed for this opportunity because I knew that you were one of the few people I could trust to judge my ability."

"And what makes you think I would want to?" Esther Wolff asked.

"I *hoped* you'd want to," Naomi replied. "I waited for the right opportunity. I want only to be able to say before I become part of the dirt that I tried to get back what I'd thrown away. It's important to me that I be known for more than being somebody else's housekeeper." She was crying.

"But you can't believe that you still have a chance at a career at your age. It's ludicrous!" Esther Wolff laughed.

"At my age I have no illusions," Naomi said. I need to know that I *could* have had a career—that the ability was there. It's better than wondering and never knowing. That's why I kept up my music all those years..."

"I hadn't the slightest idea that you were interested in music," Esther Wolff replied. "You never told me."

"You never asked," Naomi replied. "Sometimes I wished you'd talk about it to me, or even talk to me about the planning of the concert, or introduce me as your housekeeper to the famous people in the music world, who came here, but you hardly ever did."

Esther Wolff took the sheets of music off the table.

"Chopin's Concerto in E Minor," she said. "How well do you know it?"

"I've been studying it for eight weeks now," Naomi replied.

"Play it for me," Esther Wolff commanded.

Naomi entered the room as reverently as if she were entering a temple. Napoleon ran after her and sat by the bench. Placing the music in front of her, she lifted the cover and touched the keys softly. Her nimble fingers rambled through a few bars and soon she was playing as if her life depended on it. Her confidence was at a peak.

When she completed the concerto, Naomi rose from the piano and lowered the keyboard cover. She didn't speak. She knew she had played well.

Esther Wolff stood like a statue near the doors of the music room. Her whole world seemed to have been thrown out of kilter. Naomi couldn't look her in the eyes.

❖

As her final act in the Wolff home, Naomi prepared her employer's dinner of poached whitefish, salad, mixed vegetables, and white wine. Esther Wolf spoke not a word since Naomi had risen from the piano, but Naomi understood that words were inadequate for what had occurred between them.

She set the table as carefully as she normally did. While it was her last act in the Wolff household, it didn't bother her, for it was really no different than being fired from a job on the whim of an employer who, perhaps, didn't like the taste of the coffee one morning. It had happened to Naomi before.

"This'll be my last day here, Mrs. Wolff," Naomi said as she set the table. "It's best for the both of us."

Esther Wolff, sitting at the table, lifted a forkful of green beans to her mouth.

"It's customary to give your employer at least two weeks' notice," she replied.

"You won't have any trouble finding a replacement," Naomi replied, putting her belongings back into the shopping bag. "You don't require much. I've worked for much worse."

"What will you do? Do you have any prospects?"

"There are more jobs in housework than there are qualified people to fill them," Naomi said.

"Will you reconsider?" Esther Wolff asked. "You're putting me in an awkward position—I have no one to take care of Napoleon."

The posing of the question told Naomi all that she needed to know, that Esther Wolff had not and could not change, so she'd have to pick up the pieces and start over again in a new household.

"What about references?" Esther Wolff asked. "You'll require a reference."

"I'll take my chances," Naomi replied, rubbing Napoleon's coat briskly as she walked toward the door.

"Goodbye, Mrs. Wolff," she said.

But Esther Wolff did not say goodbye. She got up from the table, went to the door, and watched as Naomi walked down the path in the falling darkness. As she left the well-manicured grounds, Naomi could feel Esther Wolff's eyes on her.

She would, of course, remain in housework. At her age she had little choice. Other than playing the piano it was all she knew how to do. But she *would* have a choice in deciding who her next employer would be, and, although whoever it happened to be might plant money under sofa cushions to tempt her, there would not be a piano in the house. It was no longer a requirement for Naomi to accept the job.

1983

Beatitude

"FOOLED THEM SUCKERS," he said, returning to the living room and removing a half pint of whiskey from his coat pocket. "Spread some bread at the foot of a tree and waited for 'em to come down."

Lutie's pity was torn between the two bloody squirrels that lay on the sink's apron and her new husband Elmo who had no conception of Chicago's ordinances. It would do no good to explain to a man who'd lived sixty-eight years by instinct that killing city squirrels might be against the law. So she wouldn't try. Nor would she eat them for, in doing so, she'd be giving her tacit approval. No, she'd simply watch Elmo dress, cook, and eat them himself, suffering quietly as the aroma wafted throughout the three-room flat.

She had made some creditable gains in her year-and-a-half long-marriage to Elmo, the janitor at True Vine Missionary Baptist Church. She'd taught him how to write his name, how to dial the local emergency telephone numbers, and how, after countless trips on the Ogden Avenue bus, to find his way downtown. But lately she worried about him, especially since the tumor in her abdomen had been diagnosed as malignant. Lately her thoughts were centered more on how he'd manage in an increasingly complicated world than her exit from it.

Six months earlier, when Lutie had first learned about the malignancy, she refused to accept the fact that she had cancer. She had noticed the slight swelling in her stomach but shrugged it off as only fluid retention. After all, hadn't she been on water pills for years? In the early stages of the illness, she felt no real discomfort at all.

Elmo, studying her stomach every day, suggestively asked her if she hadn't some "news to tell him." Lutie was too outdone by the thought to be humored by the idea that she might have been pregnant. She was sixty-six years old! But Elmo said that according to the Bible, older women than she had given birth. Well, she certainly wasn't going into any record book, Lutie vowed. And after she had gone to another doctor for a second opinion and had the test results confirmed, Lutie couldn't decide for sure whether Elmo's disappointment was because of the cancer or because he wasn't as potent as he'd thought he was.

When her doctor had trouble communicating to Elmo the seriousness of her illness, Lutie volunteered to break the news to him herself. It was natural for her. She'd explained so many things to him since they'd been married.

"You not goin' no place," Elmo declared when Lutie told him. "They don't know what they talkin' 'bout. You need some healthy food, that's all. Been eatin' poor food too long. People in Mississippi never caught a lot of cancer. It's 'cause they raised they own food. They knew what they was eatin'," he asserted.

"I know about raising food, Elmo," Lutie said. "I lived on a farm down South, too," she reminded him.

"Well, you forgot how to cook it," Elmo said. "Been up North too long to remember. I'm cookin' you some squirrel stew," he said one day after Lutie had come home from her chemotherapy treatment. "It'll bring your strength back."

"I haven't had Brunswick stew since I was a girl," Lutie said. "I didn't think people cooked it anymore."

"I don't know nothing 'bout no Brunswick stew," Elmo had said. All I know 'bout is squirrel stew. Baby, it's so good, it'll make you eat yo' head off!"

"Elmo, the name for any stew with squirrel meat in it is Brunswick stew. Honey, that's all I'm saying."

"Well, I'm being straight with you," he replied. "So it won't be no surprise. I don't b'lieve in springin' surprises—trickin' people into eatin' somethin they don't want to eat. Did I tell you 'bout the time I got tricked?"

Lutie had heard the story at least once a month. Elmo's frequent retelling of the incident was a sign to her that senility had come in, sat down, and crossed its legs for a long stay.

Forty years before in Mississippi, a neighbor, without telling Elmo what it was, had asked him to sample a piece of meat to see if she had put enough seasoning on it. He was hungry, so he didn't ask what he was tasting, he'd said. For all he knew, it might've been rabbit or squirrel. But after he had swallowed it and licked his fingers, the woman informed him that he'd eaten a taste of wood rat, which people were known to eat in certain parts of Mississippi. He took pains to explain to Lutie that wood rats weren't real rats—that they belonged to a different family, but still, *he* wouldn't eat them.

Lutie recalled her struggle to keep a straight face as Elmo demonstrated how he stuck his fingers down his throat to bring the meat up but couldn't upchuck for the life of him. The laughing cook had told him that the meat was too good for the stomach to turn loose. Then Elmo showed Lutie how he drew back and, with his fist, knocked the woman onto the porch floor, breaking her jaw so that she had to have it wired. It was the first time he'd ever hit a woman, he declared, and the last time he'd eaten anything without being told what it was. But Lutie said that just because the cook told you a dish was one thing, it didn't mean that it couldn't be something else. It was all a matter of having faith, she'd said.

That morning, after he had brought the squirrels home, Elmo opened the back door onto the porch, where he spread newspaper so he could dress them. Normally, he field-dressed his game, he explained, but this time he couldn't take a chance on getting caught on park district property with the two dead squirrels.

Lutie lay on the couch in eyeshot of the back porch, watching him with work gloves on cutting the squirrels to the tailbone. The gloves, he had told her, protected him from catching rabbit fever. Now how he could get rabbit fever from dead *squirrels*, Lutie didn't know, but she didn't question him about it. She turned her head and winced as he cut one squirrel's pelt the width of its back. Pressing her hands against her stomach, she suppressed a retching impulse.

From her position on the sofa, Lutie studied every movement of the bantam, bashful man who had to muster the nerve to tell her to her face that she was a "fine figure of a woman." Although she was three years Elmo's junior, a maternal protectiveness came over her as she watched him move around in the kitchen—the same maternal feeling that her sister Frannie claimed made Lutie abandon all reason in marrying a slow wit.

The two of them had fallen out over those words. To that day, Frannie didn't even know Lutie had cancer. Lutie didn't have to explain her actions to anybody, she maintained. Having lived alone for fifteen years since her first husband Eldred died, she had longed for companionship. Just because Elmo didn't read the daily *Tribune*, except to circle the lottery numbers that he played faithfully, or just because he couldn't talk about the issues of the day like Eldred could, it didn't mean that the two of them had nothing in common.

At least Elmo loved her. Never before in her life had a man picked wildflowers for Lutie. Never had Eldred told her that she was a "fine figure of a woman" when Lutie knew she had long ago been jacketed by unwanted weight. Elmo treated her in the manner of a man who had panned for gold all his life and who had finally hit a mine when he had given up hope. So she worried about him constantly, fretted about whether or not he'd find a new mate as patient with him as she'd tried to be—a woman who would be as appreciative of him as he was of her.

Lutie watched him at the threshold of the back door as he stepped on a squirrel's tail and pulled the pelt from its body as easy as peeling a sock off a foot. Elmo always killed gray squirrels, he explained, because the red ones had too gamy a taste. At the kitchen sink she saw him cutting up a hen that would go into the stew. He had set out three cupsful of lima beans overnight so they could soak. Sister Perkins from the church had brought him a paper bag full of vine-ripened tomatoes from her garden. He had skinned them and cut them into small pieces. Another old bag who sang in the Doctor Watts choir at True Vine, and who never even spoke to Lutie, sent Elmo a bushel of corn for "ailing Sister Waters." He had husked enough ears for three cupsful and piled them onto a piece of wax paper.

Lutie knew that these women didn't have her interests at heart. They were just trying to get in good with Elmo, trying to build up credits so they could stake first claim on him when she was gone. Well, it wouldn't work. Elmo wasn't studying any of them. He had told Lutie so himself. And Lutie believed him.

What a good cook Elmo was! she thought. A much better cook than she was. He never had to measure anything. Instinct told him in what proportions to combine the ingredients. It wasn't Christian-like, she thought, for her to refuse to eat, to spurn the meal he was so carefully preparing. But Lutie had to admit to herself that it wasn't the sad-eyed squirrels so much that made her balk at eating Elmo's stew. It was her resentment of Elmo messing around in her domain, taking over *her* kitchen when she was too weak to put one foot in front of the other. Elmo was doing for *her* when she had been so used to doing for *him*. She knew she should have praised high heaven for him, but all Lutie could see was that this man, about whom knowledgeable people declared she had brought a long way, was functioning in her kitchen as if she were already gone. He didn't need her. That was the final blow, the last indignity. The only way she knew to banish the thoughts that had crept into her heart was to place the blame for them squarely where they belonged: on the devil. It was Satan who had made her feel this selfishness and ungratefulness. It was a good thing that Reverend Goodloe would be over later to help her fight him.

Elmo came out of the kitchen to join her, fluffing her pillow as she tilted her head forward. He pulled an old patchwork quilt over Lutie as she stared blankly at the wall. The quiet rumbling of the lidded pot on the kitchen stove sounded strangely like the bubbling in her stomach that made her feel so bloated. She watched as Elmo sat in the chair across from her and rolled the butt of a dead cigar along his gums. Respectful of her feelings, he had been smoking it outdoors since he knew that the smell nauseated her.

"Rev'n Goodloe'll be over this evenin'," he reminded her. He took the cigar out of his mouth, lay it on the jar-lid ashtray and picked up the *Tribune* that she had half-read earlier.

Good old Rev'n Goodloe, Lutie thought. If it hadn't been for him, Elmo wouldn't have the job at True Vine. She was thankful for him. He was a good pastor. A faithful steward, just like she considered herself to be.

"Think Rev' Goodloe'll have supper with us?" Elmo asked.

"There's plenty of it to go around," Lutie said, careful not to betray the fact that she had no intentions of eating any. She watched him write something on a piece of paper. He stared at the writing as though, like a hieroglyphic, it had some hidden message. He then folded it back up and stuffed the scrap of paper in his shirt pocket.

"What number you playing, Elmo?" Lutie asked.

"Seven seventeen," he answered. "Same number that's go'n win me the money to buy us a house an' a piece of land where we can raise our own food."

It was the same number that he played when Lutie had first met him.

She didn't know whether there was anything magically connected with it in Elmo's mind or not. Once, when the winning number was seven twenty-seven, Elmo whooped and hollered as if he'd won. When she reminded him that he hadn't, he said that at least he'd come close. Lutie couldn't convince him that in a game of chance there was no such thing as coming close. Either you had the number or you didn't.

"Elmo," Lutie said, as he folded the paper. "We've gotta talk about how you're gonna get along when I'm gone. We gotta talk about who's go'n see after you."

"You ain't goin' nowhere," Elmo said.

He was catching a cold and as he snorted up the running phlegm, the whistling sound made his head ring hollow.

"Elmo, don't bury your head in the sand. Look at you. You can't even take care of a cold. Snorting like a horse. I can't do *everything* for you. I'm not always gonna be around."

"Yes you will," Elmo said. "I'm fixin' you some squirrel stew. It's go'n knock that sickness right outta you."

He went over to the couch and grasped Lutie's hand. His short fingers were the color and thickness of the cigars he gummed. Such big hands for such as small man, she thought. And yet he'd never raised one against her. Was as gentle as a baby. She'd never have believed that he had broken a woman's jaw if she hadn't heard it come from his mouth. Maybe Reverend Goodloe could talk to him for her. There wasn't anything else she could say to Elmo. She'd given him all she could give and had nothing more stored away.

Reaching over the coffee table for her medicine, she took two capsules from a white bottle and pressed them onto her tongue. Elmo held her up as she swallowed the water he brought her.

"I'm tired, Elmo," she said. "So tired."

"Go on and rest," he said, easing her head onto the pillow. "When you wake up I'll have your stew ready for you on the table. It'll be just right for you to eat."

Lutie slept fitfully, drifting in and out of consciousness so often that she wasn't sure if the indistinct vision of Reverend Goodloe seated in the chair across from her was real or imagined.

"Why'nt you tell me Rev'n Goodloe was here?" she asked Elmo when she awoke. "I'm not even decent," she complained, rearranging the covers around her and adjusting the wig on her head.

"I didn't want to 'sturb you," Elmo said. "You was restin' so peaceful."

"I wasn't resting peacefully," Lutie snapped. "I was drifting in and out."

Reverend Goodloe came over to the couch where she lay. He was a tall, double-jointed man with pitying eyes and prayerful hands. When the congregation at True Vine got caught up into one of his frenzied sermons, the faithful sisters swooning in spasms of joy, he'd strut across the pulpit, flapping the long black sleeves of his robe like they were wings.

"I come to have fellowship with you, Sister Waters," he said.

"Elmo, get my Bible," Lutie said. "I want to follow 'long with Rev'n Goodloe."

Elmo went into the bedroom and soon brought out a heavy, ivory-colored Bible with gold leaf along the edges of the pages. After he had given it to her, he went back into the kitchen to check on the stew.

"Rev'n Goodloe," Lutie addressed him in a low voice, "I'm worried about Elmo. He's come a long way in the time we've been married. What's gonna become of him now?"

"No need of you worrying about Brother Waters," Reverend Goodloe said, moving closer to the couch. He sat on a hassock that Elmo had pushed beside it. "The Lord looks after His own."

"Reverend Goodloe, he went out and killed squirrels today. Park squirrels. He's making a stew. You don't go around killing city squirrels," she said.

"People killed pigeons during the Depression," Reverend Goodloe said. "They were good eating too."

"They did it because they had to," Lutie answered. "It was a matter of survival. Elmo don't have to. We've got plenty of meat in the freezer."

"He told me he was fixin' you some squirrel stew to bring your strength back," Reverend Goodloe said. "He told me how he killed those squirrels and how he scraped together the makings for the stew. His faith is so strong that it puts mine to shame."

"But Rev'n Goodloe, that's just my point," Lutie explained. "Brunswick stew and nothing else is gonna make me better, but I can't get him to see it. He's got the mind of a child."

"You knew it when you married him, Sister Waters," Reverend Goodloe said. "Let him believe what he wants to. It's the least you can do for him."

"But I can't sit back and let him go off on the wrong track," Lutie replied. "I've brought him a long way. I'm responsible for him. I taught him how to sign his name. I showed him how to ride the bus downtown..."

Elmo appeared at the doorway. Lutie sent him away with a wave of her hand, signaling that she and Reverend Goodloe were having a private conversation. Reverend Goodloe began reading one of Lutie's favorite passages—The Beatitudes.

"Blessed are the merciful, for they shall be shown mercy.
Blessed are the pure in heart, for they shall see God..."

He was soon interrupted by a clinking noise from the kitchen. It was Elmo using a spoon as a clapper inside an empty jar announcing that the Brunswick stew was ready to eat. Lutie sat propped up in the kitchen chair like a doll invited to a fake meal. For her, the dinner might just as well have been for play because her plate was the only untouched one at the table. She stared at it as if her eyes could make it disappear. Reverend Goodloe, exuberant at stumbling upon a free meal, ate heartily, greedily spooning the stew into his mouth.

"Haven't had Brunswick stew since I was a boy," he said. "Elmo, you really put your foot in it didn't you?"

Elmo dropped his head bashfully and continued to eat, mincing the meat finely with a fork.

"You waitin' for yours to cool, Baby?" he asked Lutie. "It's cool enough for you to eat now."

"I don't have an appetite, Elmo," she said. "I'm nauseous from the chemo treatment."

"You missing a real treat," Reverend Goodloe said. "It's so good, your tongue'll slap your brains out!"

"You two help yourselves," Lutie said. She put her hand to her chest to suppress a rising wave of nausea.

"Anybody who can cook a meal as good as this don't have to be worried about," Reverend Goodloe said. "Elmo, you missed your calling. You shoulda opened you a restaurant."

"It still ain't good enough to suit Lutie," he said.

He covered his face with his hands as though he couldn't stand to look at Lutie and her untouched plate of stew. Lutie heard the familiar adenoidal snort that sounded so much like a burst of air into an empty bottle. Elmo wouldn't show the tears that she knew were there. He kept his hands in front of his face and inhaled with a whistling sound.

"I wouldn't poison you Lutie," he said. "You know that."

"I believe that any treatment that keeps a person from enjoying food ain't much of a treatment," Reverend Goodloe said. "Eating's one of the natural pleasures of living."

Elmo didn't talk. He had finished his plate but didn't go back for another helping. Reverend Goodloe eyed Lutie's plate covetously as though he were waiting to be told he could have it.

"I know how Elmo feels, Sister Waters," he said. "His feelings are hurt. What if you spent the whole day cooking a meal that somebody you cared for refused to eat?"

Elmo took Reverend Goodloe's plate and went into the kitchen to refill it.

"It's not the stew," Lutie said in a low voice. "And I *have* been nauseous. But I can't lie to you Reverend Goodloe. The truth is I can't get used to Elmo doing for me. It hurts me not to be able to get up and do the things I used to do."

It was hard for her to explain that she wasn't used to having Elmo worry about her. Difficult to explain to Reverend Goodloe that she resented her husband, envied him even. *She* had always done the worrying in the house. *She* had been his eyes, ears and mouth for the past year-and-a-half. It had given her a reason for living. Her overwhelming sense of *duty* outweighed the need for her to love Elmo. He had been her cause. His progress had been the fruit of her good works—the works that would be her passport to heaven.

"Let Elmo take care of *you*," Reverend Goodloe said. "It's his turn now. You've got to give him *his* chance."

Elmo returned to the table with Reverend Goodloe's plate and a piece of cornbread.

Reverend Goodloe touched Lutie's hand and guided it to the unused spoon that lay beside her plate. She lifted the spoon and submerged it into the stew, bringing up vegetables and broth to her lips. Opening her mouth, she emptied the spoon and swallowed hard, like a child taking unwanted medicine. Dipping her spoon, she fished around for a piece of squirrel meat. When she found a morsel, she lifted it up, put it into her mouth, chewed and swallowed it, feeling the lump travel down her throat.

"You don't have to eat that cold stew, Baby," Elmo said. "I'll bring you some hot from the stove."

He left and returned to the table with a large pot. He ladled a steaming plateful in front of Lutie and refilled Reverend Goodloe's plate.

"Help yo'self," Elmo exclaimed. "It'll give you strength."

The spoonsful of stew did give Lutie strength, though maybe not the kind that Elmo had in mind for her. Little by little, the nourishment gave her strength to believe. To believe that everything would work itself out. To believe that she could fall back weakly and let Elmo take care of her in her time of need.

She swallowed a spoonful of stew, then another, and another, all the time reflecting about the ingredients that went into it. Lutie would ask Reverend Goodloe to pray for her and Elmo before he left. She'd ask especially that he pray that Elmo would store up the love she felt for him and, in the habit of the squirrels whose flesh they feasted on, would unearth it in the cold lonely months ahead.

"Rev'n Goodloe," Lutie said after she was halfway through her refilled plate, "keep those corn-giving buzzards away from Elmo when I'm gone. I know they're just waiting to close in after the kill. Keep 'em away from him cause I know he won't have strength enough to fight 'em all off by himself."

Elmo grinned. "Lutie Mae, I keep telling you, you ain't going nowhere," he said.

1985

A Mortgage Burning Party

THE TWINS, IRIS AND ISAAC, WERE LATE for the mortgage burning party Jerome had planned for their widowed mother, but it was no surprise to him. The two had held up the family portrait that had been arranged before their father's death, and while Jerome had forgiven them, he hadn't forgotten.

He stared at the rosewood-framed picture that hung above the mantel. His mother glowed and his father beamed proudly in the forefront; Iris stood behind them wearing a phony smile; Ike flanked her on the left, barely parting his lips, and Jerome was on the right masking his annoyance with a grin.

Although he had done everything he could to include the two of them, they had fought the ceremony from the start. Initially, he thought it might have been because the mortgage burning had been his idea instead of theirs, but later he had concluded that they had other motives for resisting the celebration—reasons they weren't honest enough to admit. If they didn't show, he planned to start the party without them. After all, this wasn't a photo session. One monkey—or two for that matter—didn't stop a show.

It was close to seven o'clock when he heard a car door slam downstairs. He went to the window and spotted Iris stepping out of Ike's red BMW. She was dressed for a party, but Ike wore a warm-up suit that matched his car and a pair of Nikes. Jerome opened the door when they reached the landing.

"I was hoping you could be here by six-thirty," Jerome said when they came inside. "I need some help with the decorations. The guests will be here at eight."

"You should be grateful we're here at all," Iris said, breezing past him, nearly stepping on Jerome's foot in her hurry to get to the full-length mirror in the living room. "We already told you what we think of this mortgage burning foolishness."

Jerome studied his sister as she posed before the mirror and combed her hair. It wasn't foolishness to him, but he had never seen eye to eye with the twins. Nevertheless, he was glad that they came. Since they had moved to Lincoln Park, he could count on the fingers of one hand the number of times he'd seen them that year.

"Where's Momma?" Iris asked. "I was hoping we'd be able to talk some sense into her about this mortgage burning nonsense."

"She's not here," Jerome said. "It's a surprise party. The invitation said it was a surprise. Mrs. Clayfield's occupying her until we're ready."

"You didn't mention a surprise," Iris said.

He had, but Jerome didn't argue the point. How many times had they conveniently forgotten—or ignored—something that he'd told them?

"Mrs. Clayfield's gonna bring her over when I call to give her the signal."

Iris sauntered over to the fireplace where, earlier, Jerome had tried to start the fire. The wood smoldered stubbornly, refusing to burst into flame. She glanced up at the family portrait taken three months before their father died. She averted her eyes and turned her back. Jerome noticed it.

Though his father was gone, Jerome still felt his presence in the household. At times he thought he even glimpsed his father's figure sitting by the fireplace in his Naugahyde wing chair. Their father's eyes were the focal point of the portrait. The serene, all-knowing eyes penetrated through to the core of Jerome's being.

"You're pulling out all the stops, lighting the fireplace and all," Ike remarked.

"I'm trying to recreate old times. When we gathered around the fire on cold winter nights," Jerome said.

"You can't bring back the past," Ike said. "Too much has happened."

"And you of all people should have had enough of playing with fire," Iris added. "Especially after setting a fire in the closet and nearly burning the house down."

"I was only six then... I didn't know any better," Jerome answered.

"Yeah. Daddy gave you the job of lighting the fireplace so you wouldn't feel so guilty about it," Ike recalled. "Said he was putting your skills to good use."

"His skills as an arsonist," Iris interjected. Jerome laughed.

"You going to throw the mortgage papers in the fire?" Ike asked.

"Folks don't burn mortgages anymore," Iris said before Jerome could answer.

"Mount Moriah burned theirs seven years ago," he replied.

"Churches—especially black Baptist churches—are big on ceremony," Ike countered. "A house isn't a church. A house represents security—money."

"What if the bank never recorded a deed of satisfaction to release the mortgage debt?" Iris wanted to know. "Burn the documents, and there'd be no proof that the house had been paid for."

"Proof for who? For Momma or for us?" Jerome asked her.

Neither Ike nor Iris responded, but Iris shot him a look of disdain that all as much excluded Jerome from the us.

"Me and Iris were against Momma's paying off the mortgage from the get-go," Ike argued. "We advised her to take the insurance money Daddy left, invest it, and pay the monthly house note out of the interest until we could put the property on the market. That would've been the smart thing to have done."

"You know Momma doesn't listen to us anymore," Iris said. "Not since Daddy's been gone."

"Daddy intended for the mortgage to be paid off," Jerome countered. "That was the purpose of the mortgage insurance. He repeated it to her before he died. Momma was only obeying his wishes."

"Obeying his wishes, or obeying yours?" Iris asked.

"Momma has to answer that question, Iris, 'cause I can't."

"You can't or you won't?"

An argument was gathering momentum, threatening to darken what Jerome had hoped would be a happy occasion. The twins had brought boxing gloves, but he wouldn't give them a reason to put them on. It took every fiber of his being to prevent it. For encouragement, he contemplated the family picture. His father's benign expression soothed him, helped him to keep his anger in check. He wouldn't fight, not matter how much they provoked him.

"After Momma paid the mortgage off," Ike continued, "I told her it still wasn't too late. I said she could refinance the property, take the money and buy a condo in a better neighborhood."

"I know," Jerome said. "She told me all about it."

"Somebody has to look out for her best interests," Ike argued.

Her best interests or yours? Jerome burned to ask him.

"You're against her giving up this place because you'll be out on the street if she does," Iris put in. "Your free lunch will be over."

"I'm against it because it's our home, Iris. Daddy worked himself into an early grave for it."

"Don't drag Daddy into this," Iris said. "You've got it as good as anybody could want it. Free room and board, free utilities, telephone...You'd be a fool to give it up."

"I earn my keep," Jerome defended himself. "I pay my way."

"Since when? When was the last time you punched a time clock?"

"I don't owe you or Ike an accounting of what I do around here," Jerome retorted.

"Well whatever it is, you're not doing it for free," Ike said. "You've got a good reason for doing it...for keeping Momma rattling around in this big house. You're not doing it out of the goodness of your heart."

Jerome could make the same accusation about their having a fit over burning the documents. He could say that they didn't care about their mother's financial security—that they wanted only to guarantee their own security, wanted to preserve any proof of their claim on the property. He could take the gloves off, but he resisted the temptation. He didn't want to alienate them any further. They had to stay for the party. People would think it strange if the whole family wasn't there for such a special ceremony.

"I've thought about the house being too big," he said. "But where would Momma go if we sold it? She's too old to be buying something else."

Neither of them would take her in, Jerome knew.

"What do you mean we? Ike asked. "It's not yours to sell."

"Or yours, either," Jerome countered.

"All I know is that I'm giving Momma the benefit of sound legal advice," Iris said. "Advice that knowing people would pay for. I've heard horror stories about what can happen when documents are destroyed."

She settled into her father's chair. No one had sat in it since he had died—not even their mother.

Ike tried another tack.

"Jerome, the building is depreciating—losing value. Momma's losing her investment. Real estate is supposed to appreciate—increase in value."

Jerome's mind lingered on the word "appreciate." The mortgage could have been retired much earlier than it had been, but their parents had taken out a second mortgage to pay for his sister's and brother's college tuition. Did they appreciate it? No. He didn't want to hear Ike talk about appreciation.

"Daddy overimproved this property," Ike persisted. "Putting in a new kitchen, new bathrooms, a finished basement. Momma won't get any of that money back when she sells. All you have to do is look out the window. Look at the rest of the neighborhood." He waved his hand in a dismissive gesture.

Jerome's patience was being tested. He was tired of parrying Ike's and Iris's repeated thrusts.

"It was Daddy's money to do what he wanted with it," he responded wearily. "Not yours, mine, or Iris's. And like he always said, 'we don't live out there, we live in here.' This is our home, not the street."

"It's *your* home; it's not mine anymore," Iris said. "I can't pretend. I can't fake what I don't feel."

A current of anger coursed up the nape of Jerome's neck, and he could feel his hair rise. A ground wire had been overridden, and Jerome reacted before he realized it.

He yanked Iris from the chair. "You faked it in that picture. Go ahead and look at it, Iris. Look at it! He held her arms, forcing her to confront the portrait.

"You turn me loose!" she spat out. "I won't look at it, and you can't make me. Let me go!"

She snatched away from him and glared in his direction as she smoothed her dress.

Caught off guard by Jerome's fury, Ike stared at him with hostility.

"You were his heart," Jerome said, pointing to his father. "The sun rose and set in you. And you weren't even at the hospital when he died."

"I was out of town on business. I couldn't help it, and you know it. I tried, but I couldn't get here in time. Why am I going over this? I don't have to explain anything to you." Her eyes flashed with anger.

Jerome turned to Ike.

"And you were late getting there, as usual. We waited and waited, and finally gave up. When you finally showed up, Daddy couldn't even talk."

"I was in training. You knew I was putting in extra hours at work, but then that's something you wouldn't know anything about," he retorted.

"I don't have to listen to this," Iris said, clasping her hands over her ears. She grabbed her handbag. "Why in the hell did I bother to come here? Let's go, Ike," she said.

Jerome sidled toward the door blocking their exit.

"You're gonna listen to this all right," he said. "Both of you. All I used to hear in this house was how proud Daddy was of both of you. He always talked about how successful the twins were. He didn't mention me unless he was asked, and then when people would want to know why I hadn't gone on to school like you two, he'd tell them ..." Jerome bit his lip to keep it from trembling. "He'd say, 'Junior's good with his hands. Junior can fix anything; you name it, he can fix it.' When people ask Momma, she says the same thing, 'Jerome's good with his hands...'"

"Why'd you invite us over here?" Iris asked. "To run a guilt trip on us? To make us feel sorry for you? You had your chance, Jerome, and you blew it."

"Why do I have to invite you to your own home—the place where you grew up?" Jerome countered. "Why don't you ever come to see Momma on your own, uninvited? Is it because of a guilty conscience? Is it because this house holds too many memories? Reminds you of how much you ...?"

"Of how I what?" Iris snapped.

Jerome didn't finish what he was going to say. He detoured down a conciliatory route.

"I know I failed Daddy," he admitted. "I wasn't what he wanted me to be. Every time I looked at him, I was reminded of it. Whenever I look at the family picture, I think about how I let him down. I still try to think of a way to make it up to him, but I know I can't. It's too late..."

"Did you invite us over here for a confession?" Ike asked. "To hear you pour your heart out? Well I'm not prepared for it."

"Why *did* you invite us, Jerome? You know too well our feeling about burning mortgage documents. You could have convinced Momma that it wasn't a good idea if you chose to. She'd have listened to you."

"I invited you over because..."

"Because of what?" Ike prodded him.

"Say it, Jerome. You've said everything else," Iris said. "You might as well get it all out in the open."

Jerome looked at the two of them. He was tentative, searching for the right words to say. Finally, he spoke.

"Iris, Ike, I invited you because you're my sister and brother, my family, and I ... I love you. I love you, and I want us to get along ..."

A nervous laugh escape Iris's throat, but in the outburst, Jerome detected discomfort, surprise, and embarrassment. He had never before told the twins that he loved them. Nor had they ever told him. While it might have been implied, understood, and taken for granted, it was never spoken in words. Jerome asked himself why that had been. He had broken the ice, said something totally unexpected, and it had an unexpected reaction. He repeated the words.

"I love you, Iris and Ike, and I really miss seeing you. I felt a need to tell you that."

Iris burst into tears at Jerome's reaffirmation. Her knees gave way, and to brace herself, she held on to the arm of her father's chair. Pitiable sobs echoed throughout the walls of the high-ceilinged room.

Jerome thought that if he had expressed his feelings earlier, when his heart swelled inside his chest at the sight of the twins getting out of Ike's car, he might have avoided the fight. They might not have had to waste valuable time suspecting and second-guessing each other's motives.

Iris poured out her tears in helpless grief the way Jerome remembered her crying at their father's funeral. He put his arm around her, but was unsuccessful at consoling her. She needed the catharsis that the confrontation had triggered. Jerome put his hand on his brother's shoulder, and the two stood in front of the fireplace, where a weak flame rose up from the logs and wavered.

"The fire's finally going," he said.

"Daddy's trying to say something, Jerome," Ike said. He regarded the family portrait. "I feel it. His presence is so strong."

"Yeah," Jerome said. "I can, too."

Finally pulling herself together, Iris wiped her eyes with the backs of her hands, smearing her mascara. She lifted her eyes toward the photograph.

"I'm sorry, Daddy," Jerome heard her murmur. "Please forgive me."

Ike embraced her when she started crying again. "It's all right, Iris," he said.

"I'd better go get the chicken I ordered," Jerome said. "The guests will be coming soon."

"No. You stay here with Iris," Ike said. "I'll go. While I'm gone, you can find something of yours for me to wear. I'm not dressed for a party."

Jerome went to the china cabinet in the dining room and took out the mortgage documents that were to be burned. He gave them to his brother.

"Make a copy of these at the drugstore. They're a nickel each. We'll keep the originals like Iris suggested and burn the copies. Momma won't have to know the difference."

Ike took the documents and left.

"I'd better call Mrs. Clayfield to have her bring Momma over in a half hour," Jerome told Iris.

"Let me do it, Jerome," she said. "I haven't spoken to her in a long time. Is there anything else you need me to do?"

"You can help me put up the banner," he said.

Iris went to the telephone to call Mrs. Clayfield.

The doorbell rang. Jerome lingered in front of the portrait for a few seconds before going to let the first guests in.

1988

The Derelict

A WOMAN OF HER BEAUTY didn't belong at the Woolworth's lunch counter in the first place, and had she chosen someplace else to eat, she would have saved herself the embarrassment, would have prevented the whole spectacle. Everybody knows that the Woolworth lunch counter on State Street is the most democratic place left to eat in the Loop. Where else could an African American waitress take your order, a Mexican cook it, a Puerto Rican busboy clean up the dishes, and a Greek counter supervisor oversee the operation so that it all ran like clockwork? No, a public lunch counter doesn't let you pick the people you eat with. That's why they have private booths. If the diner had taken a booth, she would have protected herself from derelicts like the one who plopped down on the stool next to her. But the management recently had posted a sign that limited booths to parties of two or more, and she was alone.

She was the picture of poise perching on the stool, her regal profile setting in bold relief the lunch counter's common surroundings. Hers was a loveliness that should have been enclosed in glass—a feast for the eyes but not to be touched lest it disintegrate on contact. It made her choice of the Woolworth's lunch counter all the more surprising.

It was too bad that she hadn't been encased in glass. At least then she wouldn't have had to smell the foul odor that wafted over the counter when the vagrant ambled in. And she had to have detected the smell like the rest of the diners who lined the lunch counter. She probably smelled him before he appeared, before he hopped onto the stool and folded his ham-heavy hands on the counter expecting to be served like any other customer.

The diner could ignore him all she wanted, but he wasn't going away. She could shut her eyes, cover her ears, and hold her breath, but he wasn't about to disappear—at least not before being served. She had already placed her order—the special—a Philadelphia steak sandwich. Who could resist the paper-thin slices of beef laced with succulent grilled onions, nestled between a slice of melted provolone cheese, all of it topped by a golden torpedo roll? The sidewalk poster that advertised the special stopped you in your tracks and set your mouth to watering so that you had to come in, park yourself on a stool, and put in your order.

The diner's sandwich was already simmering on the grill, the steaming onions doing their damnedest to overpower the derelict's odor. So she couldn't just up and leave without an explanation. Besides, Hattie, the waitress, whose territory ranged from the middle of the long counter to the end, had been johnny-on-the-spot the moment the diner sat down. Hattie had given her a glass of water, taken her order, and called it out to the cook—all within a minute of the customer's arrival. Not another seat was open, and there was no sign of another diner leaving. So there she was. Stuck. Seated next to a bum. The most she could do was to ignore him and pretend that he wasn't there, which is exactly what she tried to do.

"Gimme a cup o' coffee and a slice o' apple pie," the tramp barked to the cook, who juggled the rapid-fire orders with a speed that was comical. Now and again he wiped his brow with the inside of his forearm.

"I'm no' your waitress," he replied. "She be here in a minute."

"What'd *you* order ?" he asked the beauty seated next to him.

She ignored him, picking up the glass of water Hattie had put before her. She took a long, slow sip.

No doubt he could ask the question till doomsday, but it would probably only harden her resolve to maintain a stony silence.

"Cat got your tongue?" he grinned. His heavy lower lip quivered suggestively.

"The special," the diner replied, barely parting her scarlet lips and looking straight ahead of her.

"How much it cost?" the bum asked.

She pushed the glass of water aside, picked up her drinking straw, peeled the sleeve from it, slipped it into the tall glass of Coke Hattie had put in front of her, and thrust up four perfectly manicured fingers.

"You must be rich, spendin' that kinda money for lunch. Where you work at?"

After a lapse of about two seconds, she answered, but in a voice above a whisper, in a voice that only someone sitting next to her could hear.

"Field's," she said.

It explained why she had come to Woolworth's to eat. The lunch counter was close enough for her to grab a sandwich without having to go too far out of her way—a change of pace from the food the store's restaurant served. It didn't hurt that the city's restaurant critics had rated the lunch counter the best of the "cheap eats" in the Loop.

"What kinda work you do?" the derelict asked.

"I'm a beauty consultant," she replied.

"You must make a lotta money," the bum said.

She shook her head no.

"You like it?" he asked.

She nodded her head yes. Not one strand of hair was out of place on her head.

Hattie brought the plate with the sandwich and french fries, setting it in front of the beauty. "Can I get you anything else, Doll?" she asked, giving the diner a fresh bottle of ketchup.

"No, thank you," she said.

"Where's my cup o' coffee and apple pie?" the bum asked before Hattie left his end of the counter.

"We're fresh out of apple pies, Sugar. I have to send upstairs for one. I'll have your pie as soon as I take care of my other customer. He was here before you."

In the meantime, she poured him the coffee, handing him the cream and sugar. The bum stealthily eyed the comely young diner as she speared a french fry, put it in her mouth, and chewed it slowly.

"How old're you? You looks to be 'bout twenty-five," he answered his own question.

She chewed the potato longer than seemed necessary, but the derelict was undeterred. She finally answered him.

"Old enough," was her response.

"Married?"

She nodded her head, yes.

If she had expected that answer to end the conversation, she couldn't have been more wrong. She merely had opened the door for more probing. The nods of the head and one-syllable answers had widened the opening through which the bum could wedge his foot and force his way inside, invading her well-protected privacy.

"How long you been married?" he asked.

It was clear that her strategy was to wear him down, to make him tire of her slow, deliberate way of answering so that he'd give up and let her finish her lunch in peace. It wasn't working.

"Fourteen years," she answered finally.

"Any kids?"

She held up two fingers.

"Boy and a girl?" the bum inquired.

Another nod of the head.

The vagrant chuckled at the lucky guess. "How old?"

"Seven and eleven," she responded.

"Had the first one three years after you was married, hunh?"

One more nod of the head from the diner.

"Never married, myself. Had a hitch in the army. Your husband ever been in the army?"

She shook her head no.

"I served a long time," the derelict mused. "That's why I never got married. Wouldn't've been right for a wife...Maybe I'll get married one day..."

He swiveled on his stool and glanced about, as if evaluating the female prospects surrounding him.

Hattie soon brought his apple pie and rewarmed his coffee. He dumped more creamer into the cup and stirred the coffee vigorously, spilling some of it on the counter.

With a napkin, he sopped up the mess.

"How long you been workin' 'cross the street," the bum resumed the line of questioning between forkfuls of pie.

The diner held up five fingers.

She had begun to toy with the food, having decided that she didn't want it. Opening her purse, she took out a tube of lipstick and retraced her lips.

"You sho' is a pretty thing," the bum said. "Ever mess around...?"

The diner looked at the gray, matted hair, at the dulled eyes that bulged from their sockets, at the dirty face that begged for a shave, at the heavy underlip that exposed tobacco-stained teeth.

"Knew you'd look at me when I asked a question like that," he said, forking another piece of pie. "Where you live? North Side, South Side, or West Side?" he probed further.

"North," the diner finally said.

"How far?"

"Too far," she said, cutting him short and touching the napkin to her lips.

"I live west myself—at Thirteenth and Tripp," he volunteered.

The diner drank the rest of her Coke but did not look in the bum's direction again.

He finished his pie quietly, drank the last of the coffee, and demanded a refill. Hattie rewarmed the coffee and asked the female diner if everything were all right.

She nodded affirmatively.

"He ain't bothering you, is he, Doll?" Hattie asked.

The diner said no.

"You behave yourself," Hattie admonished the tramp with a raised finger. He leered at her and broke into a gravelly laugh.

"How much I owe you?" he asked.

"You know good and well what you owe me," Hattie said.

"Just kiddin'," the bum replied.

"Give me a dollar ninety-seven," Hattie replied, writing his total on the check pad. She tore it off and placed it on the counter in front of him.

The derelict dug deep into his pocket and brought up a handful of change. Counting out the money to the penny, he slapped the coins onto the counter. Brushing away the loose tobacco from among the nickels, dimes, pennies, and quarters, Hattie raked the money into her hand. When she went to the cash register to ring up the check, the beauty consultant blotted her lips again and pushed her plate away. With her fork, she played with the french fries while she waited for Hattie to bring her check. Hattie returned with it, and the diner opened her purse, removed a ten from her wallet, and laid it on the counter beside her plate. Then, as if she had thought better of it, she picked up the bill and held it tightly in her hand until Hattie came for it.

The bum said nothing else to her, staring silently in her direction. Apparently uncomfortable under his gaze, the diner rotated her stool obliquely so that her back was slightly to him. The bum seemed to be content studying her back. Hattie came for the check, and the diner straightened her stool to face her.

"What's wrong, Doll?" Didn't you like the special? Why you barely ate a bite of it."

"I guess I don't have much of an appetite," she said.

Hattie shook her head and went to ring up the check.

While the waitress was away, the diner discreetly eased the plate with the cold, barely eaten sandwich and french fries toward the derelict, and she spoke to him—voluntarily.

"If you're still hungry, you can have this," she said.

The derelict didn't reply. Didn't even look in her direction.

In a lightning-quick motion, devastating in its unexpectedness, he knocked the plate, Coke and water glasses, knife and fork to the floor, startling the cook. The crash of breaking glass and clattering flatware brought Hattie and her supervisor from the opposite end of the section. The cook stepped over the broken glass, continuing to work the grill.

"Bitch, who you think you are, snubbing me, barely parting your lips and then giving me your scraps?"

The beauty consultant neither flinched nor answered him. She opened her purse, removed her compact, and looked in the mirror, as if to assure herself that no physical damage had been done.

The lunch counter supervisor picked up the red phone to call security, but by the time the guard arrived, the bum had jumped off the stool and run down the aisle. The busboy, cursing in Spanish, brought a broom and dustpan to clean up the mess.

"Don't pay no 'tention to him, Doll," Hattie said, trying to smooth the incident over. "He's not responsible. You should've told me you didn't want the special. I could've taken it back. Would've been glad to. I'm not particular about the special myself. If I must say so, I like our liver and onions."

"I'm fine. Really, I am," the diner said.

"Let me get you something else," Hattie insisted. "I can't send you back to work on an empty stomach."

"Really, I'm OK," the woman said, but Hattie wouldn't be moved.

"You name it, and I'll have it in a jiffy."

The diner thought for a moment as Hattie held her pen poised on her check pad. The beauty consultant looked over at the empty stool where the derelict had sat.

"To tell the truth," she said, "that apple pie looked awfully good." She took two dollars out of her purse. "You don't think that a slice a la mode would hurt me, do you?" she asked.

"Not after what you been through," Hattie said, refusing to take payment. "This one's on me, Doll," she said.

"I can't let you do that," the diner objected.

But Hattie insisted. She wrote it up, went to her tip jar, counted out the money, paid for it, and rang it up. She returned with a slice of apple pie cut from the same pie that the derelict's had been cut from and had topped it with a generous scoop of vanilla ice cream.

As Hattie set it before her, the beauty consultant opened her purse and removed a card, handing it to the waitress.

"If you're ever interested in a makeover, stop at the cosmetics department, and ask for me," she said. "It'll be on me."

Hattie studied the card and smiled. "I just may take you up on that, Doll. I just may. But I'm not countin' on no miracles."

1995

About the Author

Mark Allen Boone is a native Chicagoan who grew up on Chicago's Near West Side. A graduate of the University of Illinois at Chicago, Mark is a former teacher who held a variety of jobs before finally settling on a career in editing and publishing.

In the mid-1980s he joined Contemporary Books as an editor in the educational division, where he developed instructional materials for the Tests of General Educational Development (GED) and rose to senior editor and, ultimately, to editorial director of the adult education division. In his free time, he wrote fiction, concentrating on his favorite form—the short story. On weekends, he volunteered as fiction editor for the Chicago-based quarterly *AIM (America's Intercultural Magazine)*, a post he held for more than 25 years.

Mark's first published novel *Reunion: A Novel of the New South* was released as a mass paperback by Holloway House Publishing Company in 1989. The following year, he founded the West Side Writers Guild of Chicago, a support group for aspiring West Side writers who lacked a forum in which to refine and share their work. The association resulted in the anthology *Guildworks Writings by the West Side Writer's Guild* (1996) for which Mark served as editor.

In 2005, he founded Blacksmith Books, LLC, an independent micro-publisher dedicated to works that presented a broader range of African-American experience than was being accepted by mainstream publishers at the time.

Its first title and Mark's second novel, *The Demise of Luleta Jones*, a literary mystery set in the Austin Village community on Chicago's far west side, was released in 2006 to highly favorable reviews, earning the 2009 Eric Hoffer Award for excellence in independent publishing in the category of general fiction. Its second and final title published in 2007 was *Some Glad Morning*, a novel by Irene J. Steele, a native West Sider, founding member of the West Side Writers Guild and current resident of Huntsville, Alabama.

During his professional publishing career, Mark has also worked as a journal and book editor for several Chicago-based trade associations. Since his retirement, he has been a freelance writer, editor, coach, and consultant who guides aspiring authors through the self-publication process. He and his wife Cynthia live in Chicago's western suburbs and are the parents of two adult children and the grandparents of four.